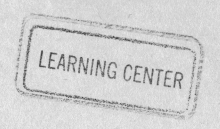

LEARNING CENTER

# OPEN ICE

# Also by Pat Hughes

### Guerrilla Season

### The Breaker Boys

## ALSO AVAILABLE FROM LAUREL-LEAF BOOKS

ACCELERATION, Graham McNamee

RED PALMS, Cara Haycak

CRASH, Jerry Spinelli

SIBERIA, Ann Halam

BUCKING THE SARGE, Christopher Paul Curtis

ERAGON, Christopher Paolini

GIRLS FOR BREAKFAST, David Yoo

TARGET, Kathleen Jeffrie Johnson

LOSING IS NOT AN OPTION, Rich Wallace

SHOTS ON GOAL, Rich Wallace

DOWN A DARK HALL, Lois Duncan

# OPEN ICE

## PAT HUGHES

LAUREL-LEAF BOOKS

Published by Laurel-Leaf
an imprint of Random House Children's Books
a division of Random House, Inc.
New York

Sale of this book without a front cover may be unauthorized. If the book is coverless, it may have been reported to the publisher as "unsold or destroyed" and neither the author nor the publisher may have received payment for it.

This is a work of fiction. Names, characters, places, and incidents either are the product of the author's imagination or are used fictitiously. Any resemblance to actual persons, living or dead, events, or locales is entirely coincidental.

Text copyright © 2005 by Pat Hughes
Cover photograph copyright © 2005 by Paul Vint/Getty Images

All rights reserved.

Originally published in hardcover in the United States by Wendy Lamb Books. This edition published by arrangement with Wendy Lamb Books.

Laurel-Leaf and colophon are registered trademarks of Random House, Inc.

www.randomhouse.com/teens

Educators and librarians, for a variety of teaching tools, visit us at
www.randomhouse.com/teachers

RL: 5.2
ISBN: 978-0-553-49444-0
November 2007
Printed in the United States of America
10 9 8 7 6 5 4 3 2 1
First Laurel-Leaf Edition

*For Paul—nephew, left wing, consultant*

*For my brothers—John, who played sports with me,
and Joe, who listened to my stories*

**OPEN ICE:**
in hockey,
that part of
the ice
that is free
of opponents

# FIRST

# 1

In the dream there's always open ice, just like that night, and he's skating hard on a breakaway, blades hissing *quick! quick! quick!* while the crowd's roar echoes in his helmet.

Raising his stick to take the shot, he catches something in the corner of his eye, a glimmer, a shadow . . . and then lights over his head, swimming, flashing, the ER, no, the rafters of the rink.

He tries to swear but the word won't come. He doesn't want to shut his eyes but shuts his eyes.

"What's his name?"

"Nick."

"Nick! Nick!"

Now he was looking at a woman EMT, who smiled: "Here he is."

"I'm okay," he said, trying to sit up.

"Easy, Nicky, easy." Coach was kneeling on the ice, rubbing his arm. "You took a bad hit. You were out, pal."

"No, I wasn't, no . . ."

His teammates milled around, a gliding gold and blue mass of worry. But Nick would prove he was all right, get up, skate away. He lifted his head; the building swirled.

"Griff?" Nick said.

"Right here, dude." Griffin leaned close, resting his blocker glove on Nick's arm.

"My head."

"I know," Griff said, a deep frown folded into his face. "I know."

The EMTs slid Nick onto a stretcher. As they rolled him off the ice, his teammates spoke, patting his shoulders, his chest.

"You'll be okay, Tag."

"Game misconduct. The asshole got game misconduct."

"Goddamn Canucks, come here and pull that dirty shit on our ice . . ."

"He fuckin' blindsided you, Tag."

"I noticed," Nick mumbled, and they laughed nervously.

"He's okay."

"Nicky Tag."

"You my dog."

"Don't miss the penalty shot," Nick warned, and their cheer spurred the crowd to echo it.

The one good thing about getting injured was hearing them cheer for you like that. But it was over in no time, and then you were alone with the EMTs and their stupid questions in the bright ambulance.

Nick shut his eyes as they moved toward the lobby. He didn't want to see anybody or try to talk to anybody, except maybe Devin. But here came his parents, calling his name, clutching at his sleeve.

"I'm all right," he mumbled, but his head was so

foggy—he'd never felt this bad before. Maybe it was true, everything Blakeman had said. Maybe all of it was true.

"Does one of you want to ride with us?" the EMT asked.

"I will," Nick's mom said.

Then they all melted into a blur; he felt sick to his stomach.

"Mrs. Tag! Mrs. Tag! Is he okay?" Devin's clogs slapping the concrete floor as she ran—that was the last thing he heard.


"He's in and out."

"I don't like the sound of *that*."

"What's his name?"

"Nick."

This was the drop pass: his old best friends, the EMTs, leaving him for his new best friends, the ER staff, to pick up.

"Okay, Nick? Nick, do you know where you are?"

He skipped to the next question: "George Dubya Bush." They laughed.

"Nick, do you know what happened to you?"

"Where's my skates?"

More laughter.

"What'd he say?"

"He's worried about his skates."

"Yeah, so would I, if I had Bauer 5000s. . . . You get 'em for Christmas, Nick?"

"What's Christmas?" he asked, and they all laughed again.

Someone rubbed his hair: "Oh, we got a funny guy."

"Your mom has your skates."

"Okay, be serious, now. How many fingers am I holding up?"

"Three."

"What state are we in?"

"Connecticut."

"Good boy."

"Any vomiting?" ER asked.

"Couple times," EMT answered.

"All right, let's vent him, get some pictures."

Walkie-talkies crackled. "That's us."

"See you, Nick!"

"Good luck, Nick!"

EMTs yelling "good luck" at you. *That* was a hopeful sign.

# 2

"Nick-oh-luss-tag-lee-OH!"

He opened his eyes; sunlight flooded the room. Nurse Janeece stood at the bottom of the bed, hands on her hips. Nick raised his hand in a wave.

"You remember me?" she asked.

"How could I forget *you*?"

"Awake. Alert," she said, grinning as she checked off his chart. "Headache?"

"Not too bad."

"Dizzy? Nauseated?"

"No," he lied.

"How many?" She held up two fingers.

"Peace out," he said, making the sign.

She sighed. "I thought I told you not to *come* back here again, boy!"

"This one wasn't my fault."

"Uh-*huh*." She wrapped the blood pressure cuff around his arm.

7

He had met her in August, when he stayed over with his first grade-three concussion, a last-day memento of hockey camp. Losing consciousness was the hallmark of a grade-three, the most serious level of concussion. Nick had never been knocked out before, and it had really scared him. Nurse Janeece had spent a lot of time with him, distracting him with stories about her kids.

"So, what do you hear?" he asked her.

"Now, *you* know I can't discuss your condition with you!"

"Well, how are my 'vitals'?" He used his voice to quote the word. "You can tell me my pulse and 'BP,' can't you? Or is that 'actionable'?"

She had her fingers on his wrist. "BP is fine. Now watch me make your pulse rate jump. There's a young lady down the hall for you."

His free hand darted up to his hair.

"No, fool, you don't want to look *good*! You want the girl to feel *sorry* for you, maybe give you a little extra sugar! Rumple *up* that hair and slide under the blanket, shut your eyes and I'll send her in!"

Nick was too proud to take the advice, and besides—he wanted to observe the approach. Devin walking toward him was a sight he never got tired of.

"Hiiiii, hun-neeee." She took quick baby steps in her heeled boots.

He reached for her; she sat on the edge of the bed and kissed him. He wondered—too late—about his breath.

"You okay?" she asked, stroking his forehead.

"Guess Blakeman'll be the judge of that. Got any gum?"

"You need it," she admitted, reaching into her purse. She popped a piece of gum out of its foil and into his mouth. "Oh my God, Nick, you got *smoked*!" She combed her straight blond hair back with her fingers. "You should've heard me screaming!"

"You? Nawww."

"Obscenities I don't even *know* were spewing from my mouth. It was like *The Exorcist*." She bent again; this time they kissed long and slow. "Mmm, that's better. Your head hurt?"

"Not this very minute."

She shrugged out of her coat and tossed it across the bottom of the bed. She was wearing her usual spray-on jeans and a cropped sweater that clung to her in most places and showed her flesh in others.

"Pull that curtain around," he said.

Devin drew the green curtain and sat again. As she leaned toward Nick he slid his hand under the sweater and rubbed his thumb across her nipple. "Nii-iick," she protested, but didn't back off.

"Wha-aaat?" he mimicked, kissing her neck, taking her earlobe gently between his teeth. She made a soft moan. He guided her hand down, beneath the blanket.

"Nii-*iick!*" This time she started to pull away.

He tried his head-injury voice: "Please?"

"Not *here*, boo."

Zzzzzip! The curtain flew back; Devin gasped and sat upright.

"You got yourself a problem there, Nicky Tag," Nurse Janeece announced, nodding at his crotch.

"Hello, *Newman*." He regrouped the blankets.

"Now when I said 'sugar,' sugar, this was *not* what I had in mind."

"Oh my God." Devin covered her flaming face with her hand. She stood, adjusting her sweater.

"How old are you, baby?" Nurse Janeece demanded, head bobbing side to side.

"Sixteen," Devin said, her voice meek.

"*Uh*-uh." Nurse Janeece wagged her finger. "Not on my

watch, anyhow." She opened the curtain all the way and started from the room. "I'll have you taken *out* of this private room, Taglio. Put you in with the little babies, see how you like *that*."

"We weren't gonna *do* anything," Nick said.

"Uh-*huh*" was her parting shot.

"If she only knew," Nick muttered, avoiding Devin's eyes.

"Nick, don't start on it, even here." Devin clicked her tongue against her teeth. "Tsss. Oh my God, don't you think of *anything* else?"

"Mmmm . . . no."

She picked up her coat, laid it back down, adjusted his blankets, poured a cup of ice water from the pink plastic bedside pitcher. "I called your house. Your mom said I could come now, and they'll be here in a while. Oh my God, Nick, they are *freaked*."

"Well, you know what Blakeman said last time."

"I know, but . . . you'll be okay, right?" she asked hopefully, sitting again. "I mean, you *can't* not play, can you, Nick?"

"No." His eyes met hers. "I'll be fine. I feel pretty messed up, though, but—"

"Well, did they even tell you, is it a grade-two or—"

"Grade-two? In my dreams. Come on, Dev. I was *out*. You saw."

"That asshole," she said tearfully.

He shrugged. "It's the game."

"Oh, screw that! It's the game, to hit somebody from behind like that?"

"He knew I'd score."

"It's not the frickin' Stanley Cup, Nick. It's a high school tournament. Would *you* do that to somebody?"

A knock on the door frame saved him from answering.

Blakeman entered, wearing a blue suit, crisp white shirt and tie. The second Nick saw his face, he knew.

"Morning!" Blakeman said with cheesy cheer.

"Dr. B.," Nick said. "On Sunday. *This* can't be good."

Blakeman's eyes jumped to Devin.

"Dr B., this is my girlfriend, Devin."

"Hi," she said shyly.

"Hello, Devin," Blakeman said. "Would you, uh, excuse us for a few minutes?"

"Oh, well, um . . ." She picked up her coat. "I gotta get going, actually. My mom's downstairs. I don't want to keep her waiting."

*Since when?* Nick thought.

"I'll call you later, Nick." She twisted his toe through the blanket. "Okay?"

"Yeah," he said, and she clicked away.

Blakeman whipped out his little eye light like it was a pistol. "So, what happened?"

"Some Canadian thug took me down from behind."

"Do you remember that? Or were you told?"

"I remember," he said. *At least I think I do.*

"What about afterwards? The rest of the night?"

"I'm a little sketchy," Nick admitted.

Blakeman nodded solemnly. "You know what day it is?"

"Sunday, unless I'm worse off than I thought."

"Can you stand up for me?"

Nick pushed the blankets aside; Blakeman helped with the IV gear. "When can I get rid of this thing?" Nick asked.

"Once it's in, we like to keep it in. Just in case we need it. Stand on one foot."

Nick tried. But dizziness overwhelmed him, and he nearly fell over.

"Good enough," Blakeman said, helping him back into bed.

"Right," Nick mumbled.

Blakeman held his arm out, extending his first two fingers. Nick squeezed them with his right hand, then his left. "Good," Blakeman said. He sat on the edge of the bed and gazed sincerely into Nick's eyes. "How are you feeling, Nick?"

"You tell *me*. You have the chart. You saw the pictures."

"Pictures and charts don't tell the whole story. You know that. The whole story is . . ." He tapped his own skull with his fingertips.

"In that case, I feel great. When can I go home, when can I play again?"

Blakeman gave his I-am-God-on-a-stick smile. "You can go home tomorrow. But—"

"Don't say it," Nick broke in.

Blakeman sighed deeply.

"Don't tell my parents this. Please, Dr. B." He heard desperation in his voice, like a little kid.

"Nick . . . remember what we talked about last time?"

"But I *can't* quit. Please. If you tell them—" He turned on his side, away from Blakeman.

"It's a grade-three, Nick."

He had to force the words: "I know."

"I'm sorry," Blakeman said softly, "but my recommendation stands."

"Yeah, thanks." Nick squeezed his eyes shut, rubbing his forehead hard. "Could you leave me alone now?"

Blakeman patted his shoulder. "Tell your parents I'll call them," he said, and left the room.

Nick pulled the pillow over his head. Easy for Blakeman to breeze in, put Nick through a neuro check and talk about his recommendation. The whole story? The whole story was that Nick had to play. He'd been skating since he was five years old, up the ladder through every level of youth hockey. As he'd grown older there had been spring hockey, travel teams, summer camp. Every season of the year, getting better, loving it more, hearing other teams' coaches say, *Watch that kid*. It was the only thing he cared about . . . the only thing he was any good at. He'd be nobody if he couldn't play.

Blakeman didn't get it: hockey wasn't just his sport. It was his life.

Nick's head was pounding. He took deep breaths and blew them out again, the way he did before a game, trying to calm down and focus.

*Don't think about it anymore*, he told himself. It would all work out. It had to.

**3**

Brian walked in empty-handed; Nick turned his palms up in question.

"What?" his brother asked.

"Wha'd you bring me?"

"I know how you love hospital food, so I—"

"Wha'd you bring me?" Nick repeated; they were both laughing.

Brian stepped back into the hall and returned with a brown grocery bag. Nick took it, stuck his head in, inhaled: Nana. "Ahhh." He pulled out a meatball sub, then plastic containers of roasted peppers and eggplant parmigiana. "Let's see . . ." He opened the peppers; Brian gave him a plastic fork from the hospital tray.

"Oh yeah, they called Grandma in Florida. She says she doesn't want to be outdone by the Eye-tal-yins, so she's FedExing a soda bread."

"Really?"

"Kidding, Nick."

"*I* knew that." After one bite of peppers, he put the fork down. "So where's the 'rents?"

"Parking. I got out in front. How do you feel?"

"I could tell you, but then I'd have to shoot you."

Brian made a face. "That bad?"

"I tried to get up, and I nearly crash-landed."

"Oh, man."

"And Blakeman was here."

Brian looked his question.

"He's all, 'Remember what we talked about last time?'"

"Damn! What'd *you* say?"

Nick shrugged. "I started crying."

"Yeah, right," Brian laughed. "You want your sub?"

"Nah. I'm not that hungry, actually."

"Dude, you *must* be sick. Can I have it?"

"Just put it down. I'll eat it later."

Brian repacked the bag and rolled the top. "Devin come?"

"She would have, but the nurse walked in."

Brian shook his head sheepishly and walked fast to the window.

They were a year apart in age, a world apart in every other way. Brian had wavy, sandy-colored hair, blue eyes and a turned-up nose, like the Irish side of the family. Nick's hair was dark and spiked, his eyes deep brown, his nose Roman—like his father's. Brian was easygoing, well-behaved, an honor student. Nick had a hot temper, a wise mouth and a C average.

Nick always thought of them as Goofus and Gallant, in that *Highlights for Children* magazine you only read in the dentist's waiting room. Goofus was the ne'er-do-well brother, always scowling. Gallant was the perfect little knight-in-shining-smiles.

"Bri, did you see it?" Nick asked. "The hit?"

As Brian turned to reply, their parents walked in.

"Hey, buddy," their dad said, trying for the no-problem smile.

"Hey," Nick said.

His mom pressed her lips to his forehead. "How do you feel?"

"Good."

She opened her huge purse and took out his CD player and some CDs. "Brian said you'd want these—Dave Matthews Band, right?"

"Yeah, thanks."

"Gabriel was looking all over for you this morning. Turning up his little palms and asking: 'Eh Nicky?' "

Nick couldn't help smiling. "Where is he?"

"At Nana's. Stuffing his face with pizzelles when we left." She glanced at her watch, nervously fussed with his blankets. Nick decided to put her out of her misery.

"Blakeman left an hour ago. Said he'd call you."

"Oh!" Turning to Nick's dad, she shook her head. "That man! He *said* he'd be here late in the afternoon! He left an *hour* ago? One o'clock is !ate in the afternoon?"

"Maybe he had a golf game," Nick said.

She was too stressed to get the joke. "There's six inches of snow on the ground!"

"Maybe it's an indoor course," Nick answered.

Still not even a smile.

Brian continued staring out the window, hands in pockets.

"Well, what did he say, Nick?" Her voice softened, and she sat on the edge of the bed.

"Said it was a grade-three," Nick mumbled.

"Well . . . we knew *that*," his father said, nodding and frowning.

"Then what more do you want to hear?" Nick snapped. "You know what he thinks."

"Oh, Nick." His mother rubbed his arm.

"He's wrong." Nick pulled away. "It was no grade-three. I was awake the whole time."

"No, honey," his mother said, humoring him.

"Well, I'm not quitting," he warned, and his parents traded glances. "Don't bother with the secret looks—I'm not quitting."

"Let's just wait and see what Blakeman says, okay, buddy?" his father asked.

"Whatever, *buddy*," Nick answered, picking up the TV remote. "How do you turn this stupid thing on, anyway? Do I have a phone in this room?"

They jammed themselves through the door in a jumble: Griff, Jamie, Steve and Ray, all in their letter jackets, talking at once, looking nervous and too big for the room, poking at Nick's dinner tray, taking possession of the remote.

Nick was in no mood. His head hurt and he felt sick and even though he'd been sleeping for—how long? at least a couple of hours—he was still tired. They peppered him with questions. Only Griff was silent.

"Wha'd your doctor say?"

"You feel okay?"

"How's your head?"

"You going home tomorrow?"

"Can you play Saturday?"

"Play *Saturday*?" Nick shot back at Jamie. "You fuckin' idiot, you *were* on the same ice, right?"

Jamie, always slow to catch an insult, continued in his dopey way: "Oh, man, Tag . . . you shoulda seen it! The guy was like . . ." He threw a body check at the air. "You flew into the boards. Your head bounced twice—off the glass, then off the ice."

Nick looked at Steve, the third member of the line Coach had named the Renegades; Steve nodded agreement. "Mac said you were lucky your shoulder hit first. He said you could've been looking at a spinal injury."

"Great," Nick said, grimacing. "Just don't tell my neurologist."

"Asshole knew he was out of the game." Ray played defense; he was the size of a Hummer, and he always looked out for Nick. "Skated off before I could even get to him."

"Him and me were having problems right off the hop," Nick admitted. "I should've expected it."

"It's not your fault, Nick." The words seemed strange coming from Steve, who was usually right there with a put-down or a joke.

"Yeah," Ray agreed. "Nobody should have to skate wondering if they're gonna get hit from behind. That's bullshit."

Nick shrugged. "That's hockey."

"Well, cheer up, Tag," Jamie said. "Maybe you'll get the sympathy blow job."

As Nick pushed out his breath in a cough, he looked fast to Griff—who looked just as fast away. "Jesus." Nick shook his head. "You people are worse than girls."

He couldn't believe Griff would talk about him and Devin. Nick had never come right out and said "Don't tell anybody," but that was only because he didn't think he had to. Griff was his best friend—they'd been skating together since mites, always on the same team, and they practically lived at each other's houses. Nick assumed what he said to Griff stayed between them. Who else had Griff told?

At least it was news to Ray. "Oh, so Devin won't, huh?" Ray was only a year ahead of the rest of them, but he patted Nick's head and said, "That's all right, Nicky, such activity would be wasted on you youngsters. It'd be over in five seconds."

Jamie, who had probably never even kissed a girl, said: "And that's a problem because—?"

"Hey," Nick said. "Show a little respect, huh? I'm a brain injury victim."

Steve lifted a plastic bowl of lime Jell-O. "Yeah . . . *this* is Tag's brain." He overturned it; the Jell-O splattered on the tray. "*This* is Tag's brain on the boards."

Nick laughed with them. "And you guys were a real comfort when I came to. Thanks. Now I know how you'll look at me in my coffin." He let his eyes glaze and his jaw drop; they laughed. "And Griff's standing there like a fruit, looking like he's gonna cry." He twisted his face, imitating Griff's nervous frown.

They all roared except Griff, who grinned and turned away, embarrassed. Too bad—it was fair payback.

"So who took the penalty shot?" Nick asked, and they looked uneasy. "You missed it? You missed the penalty shot?"

"Deke took it." Now Ray was all serious and defensive. Deke was a cocaptain—a center, like Nick, and the only reason Nick was still on the second line. "So if you got a beef about it, I suggest you take it up with him."

"*Deke* missed the penalty shot?" Nick asked, bewildered.

"He was pretty shook up, Nick," Ray said solemnly. "We all were."

"Which was exactly what they wanted," Nick shot back. "We *did* win the game, right? Please tell me we won the game."

Again, they shifted their weight, shifted their eyes.

"Shit!" Nick slapped the mattress.

"It was only a tournament," Griff mumbled. "Not like it mattered to the season."

"Great. I got my second grade-three for not-like-it-mattered."

"But you'll be back, right?" Jamie said eagerly.

"Yeah, just . . . it might be a while. Till I get clearance." Nobody spoke.

"You know . . . doctors come in and shine lights in my eyes, and if I can't recite the Gettysburg Address backwards, they say I have impaired whatever."

"They don't understand you're just naturally stupid," Steve said.

"I try to tell 'em," Nick agreed. "I said, 'Just ask my teachers.' "

"Hey, Tag—at least you get to miss Diversity Workshop tomorrow," Jamie said.

"One . . . two . . . three . . . *four!*" Nurse Janeece marched into the room. "Now silly me, all these years, I thought the limit was *three* visitors!"

"They're slime, ma'am," Nick said. "Slime. Throw them out," he added, half wishing she would.

And he knew she understood, because as she left she said: "Ten minutes, team. Then your boy needs his rest."

Nick was dozing with the Rangers game on when a young blond doctor entered with a gung-ho "Hi!"

"Hi," Nick said.

"Remember me?"

"Sure."

The doctor clicked on his eye light.

"You guys think those things are pretty cool, don't you?"

"Ah, an old hand. He knows where to look without being told. Been down this road before?"

"Couple times."

The doctor bent to take his pulse. This was unique. Doctors didn't take pulses, they looked at charts. Who was this guy?

"I just wondered how you were doing," he said casually. "After you cussed me out in the ER."

Nick recalled no such incident, but he said, "Yeah, sorry. I was pretty messed up."

The guy looked at him close. "You *don't* remember me, do you, Nick?"

Nick just stared back.

"You didn't cuss me out. You cussed out another doctor."

"I got you mixed up."

"He's Asian."

Nick turned his face. "Don't screw with my head, okay? It's got enough troubles."

"Sorry, Nick. I'm the guy who admitted you from ER. I'm on the head trauma team. Dr. Hurt."

They shook hands; Nick grinned. "Dr. Hurt?"

"I know, I know. It's H-I-R-T. Think I should change my name?"

"Unless you want to hear the same joke your whole life."

"I know. Hey, mind if I ask you a few questions? I'm off duty. This is purely . . . personal interest."

"Busman's holiday, my father calls it."

"Right," the doctor replied, nodding. "What's your dad do?"

"He, uh . . ." *He has a job I can never explain very well. Especially today.* "He's, like, a consultant."

"Oh yeah? My father's an engineer. What's your dad consult on?"

"Um . . ." Nick shook his head. "Construction. Where to build . . ." He shrugged. "How to build stuff."

"Oh. What about your mom, does she work?"

"Yeah, she works at Blue Cross."

"Really? I guess you get pretty good medical coverage, huh?"

"Yeah. The joke is, if she ever gets laid off, I have to quit hockey."

Hirt's weak smile made Nick uneasy. "What's she do at Blue Cross?"

"Customer service. Listens to people complain all day."

"Probably about guys like me. Where do you live?"

"Shore Haven."

"We're practically neighbors. I live in Rocky Creek. You have brothers? Sisters?"

"My brother Brian's a year younger, and then we got Gabriel—he's two."

"Wow! How was that for you and your brother? All of a sudden, you're teenagers, you have a baby in the house."

Nick shrugged. "It's okay. He's pretty cool. Sometimes he's a pain. And you gotta watch your language."

Dr. Hirt laughed. "You remember what my dad does?"

Nick stared at him. "No."

"Where do I live?"

Nick's heart was pounding in his throat. He hated this guy. He wasn't answering one more question.

"Remember my name?"

"H-I-R-T," Nick said steadily, glaring at him.

Hirt nodded. "Good. My father's an engineer, and I live in Rocky Creek."

"I'm happy for you. Don't ask me again."

"Nick . . . ," Hirt said in a don't-be-so-touchy tone.

"You doctors." Nick shook his head. "You think people are just charts and tests and research. Head trauma team three, patient zero." He reached for the nurse-call button, squeezed it. "Leave me alone." He pressed the button again. "Go torture somebody else."

"I'm sorry, Nick," Hirt said. "I really am." He tucked his eye light in his pocket and left the room.

"What *are* you buzzin' about, Taglio?" Nurse Janeece breezed in.

"Where were you, painting your nails?"

"Well, since you didn't *keep* buzzin' I figured, 'He's

23

either over it or he's dead. Either way, *I'm* no longer needed!' "

She caught his eye and burst out laughing, which broke him up. She had the kind of deep-in-the-throat laugh that made you have to join in, even if you tried not to. Only black people had such great laughs—but you couldn't say that in Diversity Workshop. In Diversity Workshop, you had to pretend everybody was exactly the same.

"How come you're still here?" he asked.

"I'm pulling a double tonight. Christmas bills."

"How's your son?" He held out his arm for the blood pressure cuff. "He end up quitting school?"

"No, I talked him into going back. But he doesn't like it. That boy does not know *what* he wants. I *was* hoping he'd join the service when he turns eighteen. But now with all this Osama nonsense, I don't want my boy over there scooting around in caves!"

Nick laughed.

"His school, though . . ." She shook her head. "Mm-*mmm*, sometimes these teachers make me so mad! Black and white, they're all the same. Black boy gives them a little attitude, suddenly they think they know *everything* about him. Then he's just part of the homeboy wallpaper."

Nick nodded. "That bites. He keeping out of trouble, though?"

"Yeah, pretty good. Now I hear cocaine is back. You believe it? I said to Dontay, 'Don't *you* put nothing up your nose! That crayon you stuck up there when you were three was enough!' "

Nick laughed again—but now he felt a little light-headed, and a wave of pain.

"You okay, baby?" She laid her hand on his arm.

*Engineer*, he thought. *Rocky Creek.*

"Nicky? You want some Tylenol?"

"Thanks."

It seemed to take forever; by the time she got back, his head was pounding.

"What'd you do, run down to the Rite-Aid?" he mumbled.

She snickered, setting the little white cup on the tray. "You think it's like your mama going in the medicine cabinet? Just shake a couple out and bring 'em down?"

"Shh. My head hurts."

"You want to go to sleep?"

"Yeah, I think I will."

She flattened the bed and adjusted his blankets. "You warm enough?"

"Yep. Thanks."

"G'night, then."

"Not if you wake me up every hour to ask me what my name is."

She shook her head. "Child, I pity your poor mama!"

"Me too. . . . Hey, you know what I was thinking? When you were gone?"

"Oooh, he's *thinking*! *That's* a good sign!"

Nick grinned. "What you said about the wallpaper. It's not just black kids. There's white-boy wallpaper, too."

"Oh?"

"Yeah, especially if you're an athlete. And, like, me, with my name—everybody thinks you're the Sopranos."

She raised her eyebrows, nodding. "Well, you need to show 'em, don't you? You and Dontay both. Show there's more to you than they think."

Nick shrugged. "Or not." He pulled the blankets up to his chin, shut his eyes.

"Good night, Nicholas," she said wearily. "Don't press that button, now. I plan to take a nap!"

She left laughing; he reached for the phone to call Devin. But what was her number? A wave of panic washed over him: he couldn't remember Devin's number? No, it was all right. It was just that he had her on speed dial, on his cell. He'd never even memorized her number.

The bedside phone rang, and he reached around to get it. "Hello?"

"Hiiii, sweee-deee."

"Hey. I was about to call you."

"I *just* walked in. I was at my grandma's for dinner. And before that, I went to the mall with Alyssa. Bought you a little present. What'd the doctor say?"

"You don't want to know."

"Oh *no*!" she said dramatically. "Really, Nick? Oh *no*!"

"And then this other dick comes in, 'Oh, I'm on the head trauma team,' playing his little memory games."

"How'd you do?"

"I lost."

"Oh, Nick. Oh, baby. That's terrible! I mean, you *have* to play! They can't make you stop playing, can they?"

He didn't answer.

"Nicky? You there?"

"Yep."

"You're mad."

"No, I was just wondering. When's the part where you say, 'How's your head, Nick? How do you feel, Nick?' "

Count two, then she said: "I'm sorry, boo. I was just . . . How do you feel, sweetie? Can you come home tomorrow? Nicky?"

"Probably."

"Everywhere I went today, people were asking for you. It's like, the news got around *so* fast. Everybody's all, 'How's Nick, did you see Nick?' "

"That's nice."

"Oh, Nick." She clicked her teeth. "Tsss. Are you gonna not talk to me now and be all sarcastic? Because I have a paper to write, and if you're gonna be all moody and one-word answers, I'll just go and write it."

He waited: once more, she just had to say she was sorry one more time.

"Nick? I *said* I'm sorry. Be nice."

"Miss you, Dev," he said, closing his eyes.

"Ohhh . . . I miss you, too, baby. I'll come over after school tomorrow."

"Good." He turned onto his back, shifting the phone to his left hand, and reached under the blankets. "Talk to me."

"Wish I could be there," she whispered. "I'd make you feel better."

All at once he was overwhelmed with sleepiness. It was very strange—to be in this state but unable to do anything about it because he was so tired. Somebody wheeled equipment past his room with a metallic clatter. *That* would help get you out of the mood.

"Dev? I'm goin' to sleep now."

"You *are*?"

"Uh-huh. But don't hang up. Just keep talking till I fall asleep, okay?"

"Nick, are you all right?" she asked, alarmed.

"Yeah, I just . . ." *I just don't want to be alone with my messed-up brain.* "Tell me a story or something."

"Okay, well, I went to my grandma's? And my uncle from Scituate was there? So my little cousin says . . ."

Nurse Janeece was carefully sliding the phone under his IV line. Then she adjusted his blankets and left the room.

*Engineer,* Nick thought. *Rocky Creek.*

He was all right. He'd be okay.

In the morning, he wouldn't respond to Blakeman's neuro check.

"Nick," his father said nervously. "Come on now. You're being childish."

"That's 'cause I'm a child. Isn't this Children's Hospital?"

His mother just stood there with her pinched little faith-and-begorra face, looking woebegone.

"Nick," Blakeman said, "it's important to assess your neurologic function if—"

"Blah, blah, blah," Nick interrupted.

"Nicholas!" his mother yelped.

"Have it your way, Nick." Blakeman flipped the chart clipboard down to his side. "I won't release him today," he told Nick's parents, and started out of the room.

"Okay!" Nick shouted.

Blakeman halted.

"All right, do your stupid little test!"

Blakeman walked back to the bed; his parents watched expectantly.

"I'm not doing it with you two standing there like ghouls," Nick warned.

Blakeman suggested: "I think Nick would be more comfortable if—"

"We'll just grab a soda," his father finished.

Nick knew Clinton had been president before Bush. He knew what had happened on September eleventh. He could repeat a series of four words as soon as Blakeman said them, but thirty seconds later he could only remember *tree*. He could not balance on one foot. He had a feeling he didn't ace the follow-my-finger routine. He stacked multiples of three pretty easily through the teens, but when he got into the twenties he faltered, let his voice trail off and stared hard at the floor.

"It's scary, Nick, I know," Blakeman said. "You *will* improve. But . . . do you see the difference from last time?"

Nick nodded.

"With each successive head injury, the brain takes it a little more personally. It's as if the brain is saying, 'Listen, pal, I can't take much more of this.' Not only are you slower to recover, but each concussion puts you at greater risk of yet another concussion. You took a big hit Saturday— but a smaller hit might have produced the same results. Remember what happened with the November concussion? It was only rated a grade-two, but you had postconcussive symptoms weeks later. Each time, it takes less and less to compromise the patient's neurologic function. And that's why—"

"I can't stop playing," Nick interrupted.

"And I can't *make* you stop."

"But they can." Nick tilted his head toward the door.

"And they will, if you tell them. Can't we just see how it goes in the next week or two?"

"Nick . . ."

"Lindros still plays, and he—" Nick cut himself off, but too late.

Blakeman jumped on it: "Lindros? This is a pretty dicey time for you to be bringing up Lindros."

Eric Lindros was Nick's favorite NHL player, famous for fighting, for scoring, for his head-down, bull-rush playing style . . . and for concussions. Last month, Lindros had gotten his seventh concussion and sat out four games, even though it was only a grade-one. Nick sighed. What a fool he was for mentioning Lindros.

"No, Nick. Eric Lindros proves *my* point, not yours. I'm sure you're well aware that many medical professionals believe he should have hung up his skates by now."

"I'm aware."

"And his brother Brett, you fail to mention, quit on his doctors' advice."

"Well maybe hockey means more to Eric. And me."

"You're sixteen years old, Nick. You've got your whole life ahead of you. But if you continue to play hockey—"

Nick's parents appeared at the door, smiling like uninvited company.

"Come on in," Blakeman said.

Nick's dad handed him a Powerade. "Thanks," Nick mumbled.

"We're going to reassess next week," Blakeman announced; Nick nearly choked on his drink, swallowing a grin. "I want him to rest as much as possible—no school till, let's say, Thursday, and then only if he feels up to it. Monitor his symptoms and—"

Nick's mind was on fast-forward: reassess. Not no, not never. Reassess. He *would* play again. Be more careful.

Adjust his game. Learn to keep his head up. No more concussions.

"—directly to the ER," Blakeman was saying. "Do you understand, Nick?"

He'd lost track of the conversation but agreed anyway. "Yes."

"Rest, rest and more rest. No late nights. *No alcohol*. You hear that, Nick?"

"*I* don't drink," Nick said. It was partly true, anyway. He never drank the night before a game.

"Tylenol for headache. And we'll see you in clinic next Wednesday, okay?"

Nick was in a great mood then—didn't even object to riding out in a wheelchair.

At the car he got in front, and turned on the radio as soon as they left the garage.

"Five-fifty?" he asked his father. "Even after they stamped your little card? What a gyp. Oops. Can't say that. It's offensive to Gypsies. Did you guys know that? Learned it from Ms. Dyer in Diversity Workshop. In the 'Hurtful Labels' session."

No answer.

Nick strapped his seat belt as they pulled into traffic. "Paddy wagon," he went on. "Can't say that, either. Offends the Irish." Nick turned to look at his mom. "Apparently your crowd would go out and get bombed all the time when you came here. Then the cops would throw you in the police truck. That's how it got the name paddy wagon. I pointed out that your crowd still goes out and gets bombed all the time. Dyer was not amused." Now his mother managed a pathetic little smile. "Anyway, paddy and mick—those are the hurtful labels for the Irish." He turned to his dad. "And your people are guineas and wops. But I knew that from *The Sopranos*."

31

Still no answer.

"Guys . . . I *think* you're supposed to be a little happier. Reassess—you heard the man same as me, right?"

His father sighed. "Nick, we just don't want you to get your hopes up too high."

"Oh, man, you two. What is it you're always saying to me? 'Don't be so negative, Nick. You're always so negative.' Silver lining time, people! Reassess!"

They kept up the moping, but Nick refused to be dragged down. Three days at home with nothing to do but eat and sleep, watch TV, burn a couple of CDs. Hopefully his mother would go back to work tomorrow—and there was one good angle to being sidelined: with no practice after school, and Brian at basketball, Devin could come over.

Who could say where that might lead?

**6**

"Bob the Builder—can we fix it! Bob the Builder—yes we can!"

Gabriel sang at the top of his lungs, jumping back and forth from couch to couch. Every time he landed on Nick's, it jounced Nick's brain, making him dizzier.

"Get down, Gabey. You're hurting Nicky's head."

"Bob the Builder!"

Nick grabbed for the baby's shirt, but he snaked out of Nick's reach. Brat. Whenever Nick was away, he missed Gabriel so much. But five minutes after seeing him, he was sick of him again.

"Ma!" Nick called. "Gabriel . . . quit jumping!"

"Yes he can!"

Nick clicked off the TV.

"Noooooo!" Gabriel howled. "Put it back! Put it back!"

"Are you gonna quit jumping on me?"

Gabriel snatched at the remote. Nick stuffed it under his stomach. Gabriel began to pummel him.

"Hey, hey, hey!" Their mother dropped the laundry basket and rushed to them. "Gabriel!" She lifted him away.

"Where were you?" Nick complained. "I was calling you!"

"I just went down to get the clothes out of the dryer . . ."

"Bob the Builder!" Gabriel screamed, thrashing.

"Nick, did you turn off his show?"

"He was jumping all over me!"

"Bob the Builder! Put it back!"

She switched on the set; Gabriel plunked down and planted his thumb in his mouth.

"I'm sorry, Nick. . . . I'm just trying to get a few things done around here, as long as I'm home." Her voice was somewhere between defensive and apologetic.

"Yeah, okay, explain that to Blakeman," Nick answered. " 'I don't understand it, Mrs. Taglio—Nick's MRI shows little footprints upon his brain.' 'Oh, dear me, Doctor—is it possible that's because I was doing the laundry while my two-year-old was trampling on Nick's head?' "

She shook her head, sighing. "Nick, why don't you go to bed? When Brian gets home I'll be able to take Gabe to the park for a while."

"Brian has basketball," he said, sitting up slowly. "Just take him out. I'm fine."

"You know the rules, Nick." She started to fold the clothes.

"Why didn't you just bring him to Nana's?"

"I thought I should give her a break, as long as I'm home anyway."

"Oh, good. Kathy's list for the day: one, give Nana a break; two, do laundry; three . . . hmmm, what was three? Oh, yeah! Take care of that kid with the brain injury."

"Nick, go to bed." She waved him off.

He stood. Which was spinning, the room or his

34

head? "Devin's coming after school. You can take him out then."

"Okay, Nick, I'll be leaving you and Devin in the house alone."

"Like we'd do anything with you peeking in the windows."

"Sure, Nick, I have nothing better to do with my time."

"You're going to work tomorrow, right?"

"Go to bed, Nicholas."

Devin woke him with a kiss; Griff was at her side.

"What're *you* doing here?" Nick asked him.

"Nothing wrong with your brain," he answered, laughing. "Get your ass to practice."

Nick looked at the clock.

"I know everybody's gonna ask me about you," Griff explained. "I drove Dev over so I could see if you're drooling or what."

"Cade asked me how you were," Devin announced, and Nick's eyes shot to hers. "Oh my *God*, Nick." She rolled her eyes and clicked her tongue: "Tsss. He just wanted to know if you're okay."

"Yeah, right."

"We interrupt today's episode of *The Young and the Jealous* for a special report," Griff said, holding his fist to his mouth. "We're here with Nick Taglio, who suffered a crushing—and, might we add, illegal—hit in tournament play Saturday. Nick, how are you feeling?" He offered Nick the microphone.

"I'm a little shaky, Griff, but my hopes were buoyed this morning when my neurologist said he'd reevaluate me next week."

"Reevaluate? Explain that for the folks at home, Nick."

"Well, it means he's backed off his statement in November

35

that he'd recommend me never playing again if I got one more serious concussion. He—"

Devin shrieked, covering her mouth with both hands, then threw herself on him.

"*Yes.*" Griff tapped Nick's fist with the mike. "Really?"

"Yep. I have to see Blakeman next Wednesday—but I bet I can play after that."

"Yeah, well, you better—we'll need you to beat Brock. I gotta go. Spread the joyous word. You going on-line later?"

"Yep."

"See you, Dev," Griff said.

"Bye, sweetie!" She turned back to Nick. "Oh my *God.* This is so great!"

"Where's my mother?"

"She took Gabriel to the playground."

"Because she thought Griff would babysit us." He pulled her on top of him and, as they kissed, tried to slide his hand down the back of her jeans. "Jesus, Dev. They're like a chastity belt."

"That's why I wear them," she teased.

He flipped her on her side and pushed up her top. She wasn't wearing a bra; he surveyed his options. "Hmm . . . they both look pretty tasty."

She looked up at him, her breathing heavy, cheeks pink: "Do it."

He lowered his head and obeyed; she moaned, arching her back. As he rolled onto her he thought, *She has no idea, no possible way of knowing . . .*

With a gasp, she slithered from beneath him and was gone, leaving him staring dumbly at the mattress.

Then he heard his mother's nursey voice: "Did he wake easily?"

"Right away, no problem."

"Of course, the way *you* wake him," his mother said, and Devin giggled.

"So what happened?" Nick walked into the kitchen, where Devin was browsing in the freezer and his mother was taking off Gabriel's jacket. "You saw Griff leaving and"—he exaggerated a fast, woman's walk—"'C'mon, Gabey, better get back home before those two have any fun!'"

"Nii-iick," Devin said.

"You should go on Comedy Central, Nick," his mother replied, leaving the room with Gabe.

Devin handed Nick a grape Popsicle, then leaned against the counter, peeling the paper from her raspberry one. Staring at Nick, she closed her lips over the tip, then pushed the whole Popsicle into her mouth and out again. Back, forth. Back, forth.

He shook his head slowly. "You know, there's a name for girls like you."

"Tell it to me. In my ear."

Nick put his Popsicle on the counter and his arms around her. "I want you so bad," he whispered. He wanted to say more, to insert a certain verb between *want* and *you* . . . but it might scare her. Sound too much like a porn movie.

She wrapped her arms around his neck; her kiss was all tongue. On the stairs, his mother's plodding steps, then the floorboards creaked overhead. Devin moved her hand down and rubbed him hard. But all at once his ears were ringing, his head spinning . . . everything seemed far away. "Oh, shit," he barely heard himself say.

"Nick?"

"I gotta sit down."

"You okay? Should I call your mom?"

"No!" he said sharply, but he gripped the edge of the

counter, ducking his head. "Just . . ." He started groping his way toward the living room.

"Let Nicky lie on the big couch, sweetie," Devin was saying, lifting Gabriel.

"Don't tell her." Nick lay down and shut his eyes. "I'm all right now. Don't tell her, Dev, okay?"

"Okay, baby." She sat beside him, stroking his forehead. "Oh my God, you're all clammy."

"I'm all right," he said. "I'll be fine."

# 7

Nick's mother worked till five every day, then had a forty-minute commute involving two interstates and a notorious bridge known as the Z. So usually dinner was pasta or takeout, but today she'd added another item to her to-do list: prepare home-cooked meal.

"This is great, Mom," Brian piped up, squeezing a lemon wedge over his chicken cutlet. "I wish you could stay home every day."

"*Thank* you, sweetie!"

Nick just looked at him across the table: *Are you for real?* Brian shrugged in reply and tucked into his meal.

*Gallant always compliments Mom's cooking. Goofus pushes his food around the plate and mumbles, "What's this stuff?"*

"How was your history test, Bri?" their father asked.

"Oh, it was fine. I worried over nothing."

"Tell us something *new*," Nick said.

"How'd basketball practice go?" their mother asked.

"I sucked," Brian admitted.

39

"Brian," she said, with a glance at Gabriel.

"Tell us something *new*," Nick repeated, this time looking at his brother, and they both laughed.

"Nick," his mother warned.

The phone rang. "I'll get it." Brian went to the kitchen. "No, Brian," Nick heard him say. "Oh, hi. . . . Yeah, I think so, hang on." He came to the doorway and told Nick: "Coach Mac."

Nick and his father looked at each other fast; Nick got up slowly and took the phone into the kitchen. "Hey, Coach."

"Nick. How are you, pal?"

"I'm good, pretty good."

"Well, I spoke to your dad yesterday, and he seemed to think one thing. But today Griff said—"

As Coach was speaking, Nick walked through the living room and into his bedroom. "Yeah, my doctor, he said we'll see how I am in a week." He sat on the bed. "But he wasn't, like, absolutely not or anything."

"Really? That's great news. When I saw the way you went down . . . I gotta tell you, Nick, it scared me."

Nick stayed quiet.

"And you *know* what else I'm gonna say."

"I had my head down," Nick mumbled. Skating with your head up was the cardinal rule of hockey—and the only one Nick couldn't seem to follow.

"Nick, I've got to tell you, I don't understand it. You've mastered the art of controlling six ounces of frozen rubber on an icy surface while racing around at breakneck speeds on sharp metal blades. So why can't you learn to keep your head up?"

"I know, I know," Nick said tiredly.

"Okay, well . . . I'll save the rest of the lecture."

"You mean there's more?"

Coach laughed. "Nicky, you take it easy, get your rest."

"I will."

"Is your dad around?"

Nick's heart skipped, but his sleepy brain didn't even yawn. Instead of a quick lie, he said dopily, "Uh . . . yeah."

A pause, then Coach said: "Can I talk to him?"

"Uh . . . sure. Hang on." Nick headed for the dining room. Why did Coach want to talk to his father? Did he think Nick was lying? But he couldn't ask. If there was one person you didn't mouth off to, it was your coach. He held the phone out to his father.

Standing, his father took the phone and said cheerfully, "Hi, Coach!"

Nick followed him into the kitchen.

"Nicholas," his mother said.

"Well, he's doing okay. Pretty groggy," his father said.

"I am not groggy," Nick said. "You call this groggy?"

The wop turned his back, stuck a finger in his free ear. "Sorry—what's that?" He listened. "Next weekend? Well . . ." He gave a little heh-heh chuckle. "I doubt *that*."

"How do *you* know?" Nick said. "Can you read Blakeman's mind? Can you see inside my brain?"

"Excuse me a moment, Coach." His father turned to glare at Nick. "My son's head may be injured, but his mouth is in fine working order."

Nick scowled in response as his father went out to the back porch, shutting the door behind him. *Pretty groggy.* What a dick. *He* hadn't been home all day. How did he know? Of course, Nick could just imagine how many phone calls his mother had made: *Now he's sleeping. Now he's watching Andy Griffith. Now he's taking a piss.*

"Nick," she called. "Come and eat."

" 'Excuse me a moment, Coach,' " Nick mocked in a pompous tone, standing in the dining room doorway. "A moment. When does *he* ever say 'a moment'?"

Brian gave a weak grin of sympathy.

"Oh, Nick. *Please* eat your dinner."

"I'm not hungry."

He went to his room and called Devin's cell from his. *The cellular customer you are trying to reach is on the phone. . . .* He left a voice mail. He moved to the den, which was right next to his bedroom—and even colder. The house had been built about 1830. It had charm, his parents said. It also had drafty windows, leaky pipes and cracked walls.

Before Gabriel, Nick had been upstairs with everybody else. But when the baby needed a room, Nick happily moved to what used to be called the sunroom. At night, when the others went up to bed, it was like having his own apartment.

He sat at the computer and logged on. Two years ago, his parents had finally caved to his and Brian's begging, and got Internet access. Nick had long before settled on his screen name: Nicktag. But when he finally got the chance to try for it, it was taken. So was Nickytag. So were Nictag, Niktag and Tagnick. He went back to Nicktag, followed by his birth year: taken. Nicktag52, his hockey number. Taken. Nicktag73, his number in bantams. *Do you want Nicktag73000?* the computer suggested.

Was there a better way to learn your insignificance in the world than trying to create a screen name? Who *were* all these Nicktags, anyway? Finally he'd tried for Nicktag826—his birthday—and was surprised to get it.

He IM'd Devin:

NICKTAG826: trying 2 call.
HAYDEVIN: hi baby. feel better?

NICKTAG826: who r u talking 2?
HAYDEVIN: alyssa.
NICKTAG826: Y can't u IM her?
HAYDEVIN: Bcuz I'm talking 2 her.
NICKTAG826: ha.
HAYDEVIN: A. sez rd yr mail.

Nick went to his AOL mailbox and read his e-mail from the bottom.

From MISSLYSS777: nickeeee how r u?
From CAPTAINDEKE: Whuzzup Tag?
From GRIFFBURROZ: practice suckd dont let anybdy like jerkoff genovese tell u diffrnt. mac is an a-hole i hate him i hate hockey.

Nick couldn't help grinning, shaking his head. Griff hated hockey about twenty-two hours a day, but he kept playing.

From CADERAMS: Hi, Nick. Just wanted to say hope you're OK. See you at school.
From LEFTWINGJBC: Tag u there?
MISSLYSS777 again: u r soooo lucky u missed DW. u would not have been able to keep your BIG mouth shut it was sooo stupid u would have ended up in the office! MISS U!!
From STEVEGENO613: WTF is Burro's problem? I should of kicked his faggot ass after practice. Blaming me because he cant do his job, what a jerkoff.
Once more, MISSLYSS777: nicky where R U? i'm getting worried.
From JUSTLUCAS: I know u did this 2 get out of the bio test! I heard u came home 2day. RU OK?

From ENFORCERRAY: Tag your line is already
falling apart. Better come back fast. How
u feel?

Nick opened IM boxes to Alyssa:

here now. tell Dev 2 call ME, IM U.

To Griffin:
hmm little problem betwn u and oh say a
certain right wing renegade?

To Jamie:
whappened?

To Steve:
there's a lot of jerking off going around
tonight.

To Ray:
Im good, practice was fun, huh?

Then he replied to Deke's e-mail:
my father just talked to coach, probably told
him some doomsday shit but Im fine, hope 2
play brock. Shd be @ school Thursday, dont
know when I can practice tho.

And to Lucas, his biology partner:
Thanks dude. I'm not dead yet. Probly back 2
school Thurs.

As he was typing the last one, an IM popped up from
Griff's girlfriend, Maddy.

SMALLEST1WUZ: Hi Nick how R U? That was 1 terrific hit. Didn't U hear Devin scream? I hear U R better tho. That's good of course! I missed yr mouth in DW. I have a favor 2 ask, if U feel up 2 it, wd U pleeeez talk 2 Griff, he's v. upset, sez he's quitting.

At that, Nick picked up his cell and speed-dialed Griff, but he just got the voice mail. He IM'd Maddy:

NICKTAG826: hi Mad RU talking 2 him I just tried 2 call.
SMALLEST1WUZ: IM him please Nicky?

His cell rang. "Dev?"
"Hi, sweetie. Feeling better?"

NICKTAG826: Griff what up?

"Yeah, a little."
"I can't believe how you just sacked out. Your mother totally freaked!"

GRIFFBURROZ: i suck, i hate it, it's not fun anymore, i'm quitting.
NICKTAG826: duznt answer my ??

"I was kind of bugged out, too," Devin continued. "One minute you were . . . *you* know, and the next, you're all about to faint, and then you're fast asleep."

GRIFFBURROZ: faggot genovese thinks he's gretzky, poking all these shots past me, throwing it in my face, laughing in my face.

```
then i blockd his shot and he goes nice save
griff all sarcastic.
```

Brian appeared, leaning on the door frame.

"What?" Nick said.

"Huh?" Devin asked.

"I was talking to Brian."

"Oh. Hi, Bri!"

"Uh . . . you gonna be much longer?" Brian asked.

"I just got on. What do you want?"

"I have to look something up. You know . . . home-work?"

"Hmmm, homework. You mean when teachers try to get you to do their job on your own time?"

Devin giggled.

"C'mon, Nick." Brian frowned, stuffing his hands in his pockets.

"Fifteen minutes."

"Five."

"Ten."

"Okay." Brian launched himself from the door.

"Shut it!" Nick called. "Jesus," he mumbled to Devin.

"What's going on with Griff?" she asked. "I just got an IM from Maddy."

"I don't know. Some moody goalie shit."

"Tsss. You're so *mean*."

Nick IM'd Griff:

```
Take a deep breath, u always do this. Sat
nite u'll make some hotshot save and be all
happy again.
```

And Steve:

The 2 of u fight like a pair of girls. Get
off him, y don't u?

"Oh my God, you get me off the phone and then just
start IM'ing people!"

"No, I'm—"

"I can *hear* you typing, Nicky. . . . Fight like a pair of
girls? Huh?"

"What?"

"Oh. Oh, you meant to send this to Steve, baby."

"I sent you Steve's message?"

" 'The two of you fight like a pair of girls,' " she recited. " 'Get off him, why don't you?' Oh, Nicky, that's
*sweet*."

"Sweet," he mocked, but his face was burning. How
had *that* happened? He never got his boxes mixed up. Did
he send anyone else the wrong IM? He looked at the
screen. The words blurred. "Shit." He rubbed his eyes.

"What's wrong?"

He logged off fast. "Tell Griff I had to get off. Brian
needs to use it."

"Nick, are you okay?"

"Yeah. I'm gonna go lay down." He got up, nearly fell,
grabbed for the edge of the desk. His cell skittered across
the floor, ricocheting off the wall like a loose puck in the
corner . . . and Brian was there, his arms under Nick's,
holding him up.

"Nick? Nick? I'm getting Dad."

"No!" Nick whispered fiercely. "I'll kill you!"

"Okay, okay . . ."

Nick lowered himself back onto the desk chair, pointing
to the phone. Brian picked it up. "Devin? . . . Yeah, hi. No,
he's . . . he's okay, I think."

"I'll call her later," Nick mumbled, squeezing his eyes shut. *Stop the room, I want to get off.*

"He says he'll call you later. Okay. See you." Brian put the phone on the desk. "I better get Mom and Dad."

"I'm all right. Do me a favor, get my ice pack and a couple Tylenol. I think I should just get some sleep. I didn't sleep enough today."

"Mom said you slept all day."

"Oh, what does *she* know?" Nick snapped. "All she did was eat M&Ms and let Gabriel jump all over my fuckin' head."

"Okay, okay," Brian said. "I'll be right back."

Nick did a self–neuro check: recite the months of the year in reverse order. "December," he muttered. "November . . . October . . ." He paused. "September, October . . . Oh, face it, Taglio." He rested his head on the desk. "You're fucked."

Outside the back door, Devin held the *Courier-Journal* to the window. "You're in the paper!" she announced gleefully.

"Great," he said, pulling the door open. He took the newspaper, slapped it on the counter and tugged at her jeans till the fly snaps popped.

Her eyes widened. "Nii-iick!"

"Nobody's here. Come on." He took her by the hand and headed for his room.

"Nick*eee*! Where's your mom?"

"All will be explained." He flopped down on the bed and pulled her onto him. "I convinced her to go to work. They're taking turns calling me. Brian's at basketball. We're alone, baby," he finished in a suave-bachelor voice, and she giggled.

"But what if—"

"No. Shh. No bad karma. You'll make him wilt." He worked her jeans below her knees, then snapped her thong. "Doesn't this thing give you an eternal wedgie?"

She laughed.

"I mean, what *is* the point?"

"The point"—she kicked off her jeans—"is showing your boyfriend this." She knelt over him, moving her hips like an HBO lap dancer.

"If *that's* the point, you should make it more often."

But when he drew her close and rolled on top of her, she panicked. "Nick!"

"Okay, okay."

"I'm not ready."

He flipped onto his back. "Okay."

"Are you mad?"

"No, just . . ."

She kissed his neck. "I'm sorry. I shouldn't've done that."

"It's okay."

"Can we just do the usual?"

He gave her a smile, squeezing her hand. "Yeah."

"Do you want to be first?"

"I like it when you're first," he said into her ear. "It gets me hot when you go, 'Nnnhhh. Nnnhhh.'" He imitated her moan, nibbling on her earlobe.

She guided his hand down.

*You have no idea,* he was thinking. *No idea . . .*

Afterward, she was pouty and quiet.

"What's wrong?" Nick finally asked.

"I'm mad. At myself. Because I can't . . . or won't. Whatever."

"Maybe you're frigid," he teased.

"Huh?"

"Oh, it's like this fifties word. Women who can't, you know, come." He kissed her shoulder. "Obviously does not apply."

"Well then, what's *my* problem?"

"You're asking *me*?"

"Who should I ask?"

"I don't know—Alyssa."

"Oh, she thinks I'm crazy. She's been doing it since she was fourteen. She says the longer you wait, the harder it gets."

"Should I just skip over that double meaning?"

Devin stared at the ceiling, twisting the ends of her hair.

"Maybe you don't love me," Nick said.

"Shut up."

The back door slammed.

"Shit!" In one leap he was at the window. No cars. Okay.

"Nick?" came Brian's voice, and growing closer: "Nick?"

Devin was struggling into her jeans.

Nick threw a body check at the door and sang out: "Don't come iii-iiin."

"Oh," Brian said. Deadpan, he added: "Naughty naughty." Then, imitating their mother: "If you're well enough for *that*, young man, you're well enough for school!"

"What are *you* doing here?" Nick was laughing, but his head was spinning.

"Mom sent the office lady to track me down at basketball."

"Why?"

"Did you hear the phone ring?"

"No."

"And did you turn off your cell?"

"Yee-aaaah," Nick admitted as the picture came into focus.

"And are they checking on you every half hour?"

"Shit," Nick mumbled. "Well, call her and tell her I'm fine."

"Can't. She's in her car, and her cell died. Wrap it up,

kiddies!" Brian added cheerily, his voice fading: "The Mother of Doom is on her way!" The back door slammed again.

Devin sank down on the edge of the bed, sighing dramatically. "Oh my *God*."

Just before Nick rushed her out the door, she stuffed the newspaper into his hands. Back in bed, he started to read the article in the high school sports section, headlined:

### MONTREAL TAKES TOURNEY
The New England/Eastern Canada High School Ice Hockey Tournament ended Sunday, with the Montreal Bears emerging as winners. The postholiday event, hosted

Nick skipped ahead to find his game:

On Saturday night at Northtown Rink, Shoreline High lost a heartbreaker to the Quebec Nighthawks. The upset was compounded by a head injury to Cougar all-star center Nick Taglio. Taglio, a sophomore, was brought down from behind by Etienne Geaudrault, a move that earned the Quebec defenseman a game misconduct penalty.

*So that's his name*, Nick thought. *Look at it again. You'll forget it in thirty seconds.*

The penalty must have seemed slight compensation to Taglio, who was "knocked cold" by the hit, according to Cougar coach

Thomas MacPherson, and taken to Yale–New Haven Children's Hospital, where he remained until Monday.

The Cougars couldn't bounce back after the second-period incident, losing the two-goal lead Taglio had secured almost single-handedly with a screen shot in the first period and a slap shot from the slot two minutes into the second.

"We were rattled, no question," said co-captain John "Deke" Connelly, who missed the penalty shot resulting from Taglio's injury. "We were mad, and worried about Nick, and unfortunately we allowed them to get the better of us."

"It was dirty hockey," added Cougar defenseman Zach Landau, cocaptain. "If that's the way they win up there, no wonder their record's so good."

Shoreline had trouble controlling the puck, even on the power play, and Quebec harassed goaltender Griffin Burroughs, relentlessly banging away to rack up four unanswered goals in 15 minutes of play.

"There was traffic in his crease the rest of the night," MacPherson said. "Griff was like an acrobat out there, but there's just so much a goalie can do when his teammates can't seem to get the puck out of their zone."

"Griff, *why* are you complaining about Mac?" Nick muttered.

In the final minute of the game, senior Cade Ramsey, filling in for Taglio, managed to flip the puck into the Quebec net with a rebound assist from left winger Jamie Chamberlain. But it was too little, too late: Shoreline lost, 5–3.

" 'Filling in for Taglio.' " Nick flung the paper down in disgust. "More like dancing on Taglio's grave."

His mom's car screeched into the driveway; he stuffed the paper under his mattress and faked sleep. She busted into the house, rushing to him.

"Nick?" Her cold hand soothed his aching forehead. "Honey?"

When he opened his eyes to see her terror-struck face, he actually felt a little guilty.

**9**

"**N**ick." His father shook him by the shoulder. "Come on, buddy, wake up."

"I'm up."

"Can you tell me what day it is?"

"No. Go away."

"Come on, buddy. You have an appointment with Dr. Blakeman."

"*What*?" Nick opened his eyes; he knew a week hadn't passed.

"I called him, Nick. I want him to see you today."

"Why?" Nick barked, and before waiting for the answer: "No!"

"Mom and I are uneasy about your symptoms, and the—"

"Rest, he said! Sleep! I'm resting. I'm sleeping. Get out!"

"Look, you heard him say if there were any problems, you were to come right to the hospital! Now, if you want us to even *contemplate* allowing you to play again, you'll do as I say!"

"Oh, what's this, blackmail?"

"Nicholas, get dressed!" The wop marched toward the door.

"Bite me," Nick mumbled, throwing back the blankets.

Blakeman's waiting room was always a cheerful experience. Nick sat there like an ungrateful dick while little kids with big problems played, or cried, or sat listlessly on their parents' laps. Usually when he saw them, he resolved to be a better person. But not today. He was too mad.

His parents waited till he sat down, then plunked themselves one on each side, guarding him like he was the American Taliban.

"Rest," he mumbled. "Sleep. That's what I heard him say. Can I rest here?" He looked around. "Where's a bed?"

"Nick," his mother said wearily.

"We'll get you admitted, okay?" his father said. "Then you can have a bed."

"Mike," she added.

Nick moved to a chair across the room. By the time they were finally called, his head was pounding. Now for another hour alone with his parents, in an even smaller room, sitting on the exam table. And he'd forgotten his CD player, so he was forced to listen to their mindless chatter instead of Dave Matthews.

Her: "Did you see that CL&P bill, by the way?"

Him: "Yeah. Unreal."

Her: "What was the rate hike?"

Him: "Twenty-seven percent."

Her: (Gasp) "Now who's gonna give *us* a twenty-seven percent increase?"

Him: "Yeah, no kidding."

They let about ten seconds go by in blissful silence.

Him: "Oh, did you know your emissions sticker's expired?"

Her: "Damn. I do this every year. It always gets past me, with Christmas and tournaments. . . . I wonder if I can get it moved to another month."

Him: "I doubt it. But who knows? You could ask."

Her: "You sit in that damn line your whole lunch hour. Just one more way for the state to take your money and waste your time."

Him: "Well, I'll do it for you. It won't kill me."

Her: "Oh, honey, you're so romantic. . . ."

Them: (Giggle, giggle)

"God, spare me!" Nick burst out.

They stared as if he'd just dropped through the ceiling.

"It's bad enough you dragged me here for no reason. Do I have to listen to your drivel, too? It's like Chinese water torture!"

"Why don't you lie down?" his father asked.

Nick was dying to do just that—but he wasn't about to show them. His mother started reading a *People* magazine with a blond prince on the cover. His father took out his Palm Pilot and started poking away.

"What's the point of you both being here?" Nick grumbled. "I know you're salivating to hear bad news, but—"

"Nick!"

"Just think, one of you could *double* your pleasure. Hear it, then get to tell it."

"Ignore him, Kathy," his father advised without lifting his head.

"I know, I know," she sighed. "Someday I'll learn."

Blakeman finally entered in his standard blue suit and crunchy shirt, trailed by one of his pet residents in a white coat. Warm fuzzy greetings all around.

"What brings you here, Nick?" Blakeman whipped out his eye light.

"Ask them."

"Well, *I'm* asking *you*."

"Well, *I* don't *know*," Nick replied, mocking his jovial tone.

Blakeman signaled the resident, who had a go with his little light. Was that how they initiated a new neurologist—present him with an eye light? *You are now a sacred member of the neurologists club. Go forth and aggravate.*

"He's been difficult to wake," the wop offered in his monsignor voice.

"Bullshit," Nick said.

"He's had a lot of pain."

"Lie number two."

"He's been very dizzy, unbalanced—"

"How would *you* know?"

"—even though he thinks he's hiding it from us."

*Goofus conceals important medical information. Gallant always tells Mom and Dad what they need to know.*

"And, as you're witnessing, his behavior seems even more inappropriate than usual."

*Score*, Nick thought. *And screw you.*

With grim concentration, Blakeman did the crystal-ball stare into Nick's eyes. Then he started peppering him with questions: Nausea? Vomiting? Confusion? Problems with balance? Stiff neck? The headache—sharp or dull? Squeeze my fingers. Stand on one foot. Now close your eyes. Follow my finger. . . . Nick half expected him to pull a Three Stooges stunt, doing the chin thing and then swatting his nose. *You see this? Watch out for that!*

At last Blakeman let him sit down again. His mother must have felt a little sorry for him, because she piped up: "The thing is, I'll say one thing, he's not, uh, he doesn't seem to be having any problem with, um, what I think you call cognitive function."

Blakeman gave her a sort of patronizing, isn't-that-cute smile; Nick wanted to deck him. "What do you mean, Mrs. Taglio?"

"Well, I mean, he's not all spaced out and 'huh?' He's pretty quick with his remarks." She snapped her fingers. "Right there with an answer, and, um, even pretty funny. Sometimes. *That's* sort of a good sign, isn't it?" she finished in a small, hopeful voice, and Nick managed to turn up a corner of his mouth when she caught his eye.

"Yes. Yes, it is," Blakeman agreed, drawing his light again. "But come over here, both of you. Look at his pupils. Does anything strike you?"

"That one looks bigger," his father said, pointing.

"I'm not comfortable with that." Blakeman holstered the light. Then he started tapping his fingertip on Nick's skull. Temple. Forehead. Other temple. All over. Hard. Fast. First with one hand, then both. Not explaining. Not saying a word. Just tapping. Again. Again. Again. Just when Nick was about to grab for his throat, Blakeman stopped. Stared at Nick. Turned to the resident and said, "What's your thinking?"

The guy looked like a deer in the middle of the Merritt Parkway at midnight.

"Uh . . . I . . . well . . . possible subacute subdural hematoma?"

When Blakeman nodded approval, Nick's mother let out a little squeak. This couldn't be good. With her job, she *did* know medical jargon.

Blakeman said quickly, "Now, I know that sounds frightening, but I want you all to understand two things. One, the chances are slim, but two, if that is indeed what's happening, the sooner we treat it, the better."

"What's the treatment?" Nick's father asked, frowning.

"Well, let's get through diagnosis first, then if we need to we'll discuss treatment," Blakeman said with his oily smile.

"What's the treatment, Doctor?" his father insisted.

"If indeed this type of hematoma is present," Blakeman said slowly, "surgical intervention is commonly indicated."

"Oh my God," Nick's mother breathed.

But Nick laughed out loud. *Doctors. Never say "operate" when you could say "surgical intervention is commonly indicated."*

"It's purely precautionary at this point," Blakeman went on, "but I'm going to order a cranial CT scan. I'm not expecting to diagnose hematoma, but to rule it out. With Nick's history, I'd be remiss if I left this stone unturned." He said to the resident, "Ask Rosalita to find out when they can fit in a cranial with contrast."

The resident nodded and left. Blakeman put a fatherly hand on Nick's shoulder.

"Nick, what we're talking about here is subdural—that is, below the brain's outer covering—hematoma, which is basically a mass or collected pool of blood." He balled his hand into a fist. "As the hematoma enlarges"—he slowly opened the fist—"the pressure inside the head gets worse. So a person who's had a head injury might *seem* to be doing better at first, but then the symptoms could get worse, or new ones might develop."

Nick only nodded. If there was no hematoma, what was the reason for the symptoms? But if he had a hematoma, at least surgery could cure it. No more symptoms. Then he could play.

Hoping for a hematoma. Wishing for brain surgery.

How fucked up was that?

✳ ✳ ✳

Nick's current best friends stood at his side as he lay on the CT scan table. The woman was injecting contrast dye into his arm, which made him hot and itchy all over. The guy was trying to distract him, as if he was five years old.

"Man walks into the doctor's office with his dog. Says, 'Doc, there's something wrong with Rover. He sleeps all the time, won't eat—it's just not like him. He's usually an active, playful pup.' Doctor checks the dog's heart, breathing, you know, gives the dog a shot."

"Shines a light in his eyes," Nick added.

"Yeah, the whole nine yards. Nothing. Dog just lies on the table. So the doctor goes to a closet, takes out a cat. When he passes the cat over the lethargic dog, the dog jumps up, the doctor drops the cat, and the dog chases the cat down the hall, barking and howling. Man says, 'Doc, that's amazing! You cured Rover!' Doctor says, 'Yes, that'll be six hundred dollars.' Guy says, 'Six hundred dollars! Are you crazy? What for?' Doctor says, 'A hundred for the office visit, and five hundred for the cat scan!' "

"Okay," Nick said. "That was good."

"I got a grin out of you, anyway. Not *quite* a laugh, but I'll take it. When you came in here you were so grumpy, I didn't think we'd *ever* see a smile."

"Yeah, well, *you* spend three hours waiting around with my parents, then see if you're Grumpy or Happy or Dopey or what."

"When I was sixteen, I thought my parents were the stupidest people on earth," the guy said. "When I was twenty-six, I was amazed by how much the old folks had learned in ten years."

"Mark Twain," Nick mumbled.

The guy snapped his fingers. "How'd you know that?"

"Actually, he never said it," the woman put in. "It's

always attributed to him, but scholars can't find it in any of his lectures or writings. . . . We're only waiting for the dye to take effect. You know the drill, right? About lying still?"

"Yeah."

"You breathing okay?"

"Yep. Kind of skin-crawly, but I've had that before."

"Anything else?"

"Just really sleepy."

"Sleepy? Well, that's a new one."

The guy said, "Hey, if *you* had to wait for three hours with his parents, you'd be Sleepy, too." He poked at Nick's arm. "Huh? Huh?"

"*Very* good," Nick admitted.

Laughing, the woman gently rested her hand on his head. "Nick, if you can sleep, sleep. I can't think of an easier way to get through a scan."

He closed his eyes. Soon the table was slowly moving into the machine. Nick was only vaguely aware of the scanner's hum as it took picture after picture after picture, slicing and dicing his brain.

# 10

When the CT scan turned out all right, Nick was determined to show he *was* all right, and went back to school Thursday even though his parents wanted him to stay home and rest.

But the day was a disaster. He'd always had a hard time following geometry, and now he'd missed three days of a new section on theorems and proofs. Hopelessly lost, he zoned out, drawing little stars in his notebook. Mrs. Chase didn't call on him, but she handed him a folder with all the homework he'd missed. So did his biology teacher, Mr. Shunk. And Mr. Polinowski gave him the new book they'd started in language arts—*The Old Man and the Sea*, by Ernest Hemingway. He told Nick to try to read a few pages over the weekend.

After class, Nick and Lucas started walking to the caf together. Lucas was one of those kids who actually read books. "Any good?" Nick asked, fanning the pages.

"It is good and clean and pure," Lucas said solemnly.

"Huh?"

"Hemingway joke."

"You know Hemingway jokes? You're a wild man, Lucas."

Lucas laughed. "Anyway, the book's short, so *you'll* like it."

"No, I'll like the Internet summary."

"Nick . . . you think you'll read *one* book before we graduate?"

"It's actually a long-term goal of mine."

They were in the cafeteria line now. "How you feeling, anyway?" Lucas asked.

"Okay. Head hurts a little."

"Mouth seems fine."

"Now you sound like my father."

"Save me."

They paid for their lunches. Lucas went to sit with his friends, and Nick set his tray down on the team's table.

After lunch, Señora Silva gave him four pages of Spanish exercises to catch up on. Ms. Dyer piled on a study sheet for next week's test on the Bill of Rights for We the People, the class that combined American history with the dreaded Diversity Workshop.

The fog rolled in as Nick nearly fell into his homeroom chair at the end of the day. Why was everybody so loud? Why was the sun so bright? He leaned his elbow on the desk, forehead in his palm. Over the PA, the principal droned announcements.

Nick couldn't wait to get home, take some Tylenol, crawl into bed. He had Mr. P. for homeroom, too. After the bell, Mr. P. met Nick at his desk. "You okay?"

"Yeah. Just beat."

"Maybe you came back too soon."

"Maybe," Nick said, feeling like an old man as he shuffled toward the door.

"You don't take the bus, do you?" Mr. P. called out.

"Nah—I only live a few blocks away."

"Is, uh, your mom coming to pick you up?"

"She's working."

"Can you get a friend to drive you home?"

"I'm okay, Mr. P. Thanks, though. See you."

"Take care, Nick."

At the door Nick turned, hoping Mr. P. would be back
to grading papers or whatever it was teachers did at their
desks after school. But Mr. P. was just staring after him
with knitted eyebrows.

Nick dropped back from the goal.

Up on the scoreboard, another point for the grim, concerned adults.

# 11

The team skated out to Ozzy Osbourne's "Crazy Train"; Deke and Zach glided side by side, talking. Griff put his water bottle on the net and started doing his stretches. Steve sprinted down the ice, and Jamie playfully swung his stick at Ramsey, both of them laughing.

Nick huddled in his letter jacket beside Devin in the stands.

"You should be down there," Devin said. She was right. The rule was, injured players came to the building in shirt, tie and team windbreaker, and sat behind the bench.

"Mac doesn't even know I'm here," Nick replied. Now Griff was joking with Ramsey, too. *Get to work*, Nick thought sourly.

His parents came in and went to sit with the others. His mother kept shaking her head: *You don't know what I've been through*. His father talked with his hands, which kept darting up to his own head as he spoke about Nick's.

"It's freezing in here," Nick muttered, and Devin burst out laughing.

"Did you hear that?" She nudged Alyssa, who was sitting on her other side, and Maddy, below them. "He's complaining about the cold!" As they all started teasing him, Devin put her arms around him and pulled her hood over her head to kiss him. She knew he didn't like public displays, especially when parents were around. But it didn't seem wise to complain when negotiations were at such a delicate stage. He kissed her, but then gently pulled away, taking her hand.

Now his mother was scanning the crowd. When her eyes met his she looked puzzled: why wasn't he with the team? She waved.

"Hi, Mrs. Tag!" Devin called, but Nick turned his face.

They'd argued earlier, when he said he was going out after the game. His parents wanted him to come straight home, but he felt a lot better today, and he thought it should be his decision. Back, forth, back, forth, until they said, "Okay, but we want you home by eleven." And it started up again, till he wore them down to his usual midnight curfew. Then they all had to pretend *he* was making a concession, too, by promising not to go in any car but Griff's—who Nick always went with, anyway. Griff was the only kid they trusted, just because they'd known him forever and they were friends with his parents.

Nick was so sick of relying on other people for transportation. In a few months, he would get his license—not that his parents would ever trust *him* to drive at night. And not that he'd want to drive either of their cars, anyway. She had a '95 Voyager with peeling paint, and his idea of a sporty sedan was a '97 Chevy Cavalier. At least Griff got to drive a Honda Civic. Nick was going to save for a Jeep. But how he'd manage that, he had no idea.

The game began with the Cougars losing the face-off—and Nick wishing he'd stayed home. It killed him to see Ramsey taking his place on the line, ticked him off every time Jamie or Steve passed to him. Ramsey was such a mediocre player, third line in his senior year. But his grades and SATs were high, and his parents had money—so he'd probably skate at some expensive college with a terrible team.

Now Steve made a perfect—*perfect*—backhanded pass from behind the net to Ramsey, who flipped the puck right over the goalie's stick hand for the score.

The two of them raised their arms and sticks and skated to each other, grinning, as Devin and the rest of the girls leaped to their feet, screaming.

"All right!" Nick forced himself to yell, clapping.

A few rows over were Ramsey's supposed girlfriend and her friends, who went to Precious Blood, a Catholic girls' school. Funny—she didn't look especially thrilled by his feat. She clapped. She tossed her head, casually flipped back her hair. *Somebody else who's not impressed by him*, Nick thought. Or maybe she was just more impressed with herself. Snobs on the Hill, the Precious Blood girls were called.

The team looked pretty good for a while, but then Tompkins got the puck in Shoreline's zone and kept it there, taking shot after shot on Griff with almost no opposition. Nick was getting more and more agitated, bouncing on the balls of his feet.

"Come on, come on," he muttered. "Clear the slot."

Maddy turned and hugged his knees for support, hiding her eyes.

Finally Jamie managed a poke check, scooting the puck

to Ramsey, but a Tompkins defenseman intercepted, turned it right back around and passed to a winger, who skated in, wristed a shot and—score! Right through the five-hole.

Tompkins celebrated, their fans screamed, and the Cougars changed it up for the face-off. Griff squirted water down his back and in his face, skating his crease, fuming.

"Damn!" Maddy said. Nick patted her head.

From there things got worse. They couldn't seem to hang on to the puck, and they had no jump in them when they lost it. Tompkins was known for its passive playing style and use of the neutral-zone trap. Tonight the Cougars were unable—or unwilling—to force them into a physical game.

Nick's stomach was in knots. His teammates' passes were too slow. They were losing every face-off. They couldn't break the trap. They weren't finishing their checks. He could actually feel his muscles twitch with the longing to take a couple of deep strides and knock somebody into the boards. It was like being in the penalty box—no, worse. At least when he was in the box, he knew he'd be out soon, getting revenge.

As the minutes passed, Griff dug himself a deeper and deeper hole, giving up two more goals. From the time they were eight, this had always been Griff's way. When he was on his game, there was no stopping him. But if the other team slipped one in that he thought he should have had, Griff would get so down on himself, he'd lie down and die. These were the times when Nick would skate over and try to pep-talk him, joke with him a little.

"He needs you, Nick," Maddy said sadly when Mac pulled Griff and the scrubs skated out to warm up the backup goalie.

"What he needs is to believe in himself," Nick answered.

"Go down and talk to him," Maddy urged; Nick shook his head.

Griffin yanked off his helmet and sat on the bench, hanging his head, elbows on his knees. When Ramsey came off his shift he spoke to Griff, ruffling his hair. Griff nodded but didn't look up.

"You should be down there," Devin whispered sternly.

"Be quiet, Dev" was his only reply.

Nick had sat out games before, but always with total confidence that he'd be back on the ice. This was different. This was agony. By third period, his head was aching, his eyes burning. He wished he hadn't fought so hard for his postgame freedom. What he really wanted to do was go home and get in bed.

But that was out of the question. He couldn't give his parents the satisfaction—or show them how bad he was feeling.

The score was 3–2 now, Griffin back in goal. Finally, there was some fire on the ice, the skating faster, the moves more daring. Players took chances that ended in penalty calls, and the power play shifted from Tompkins to Shoreline, with nobody able to score.

This was Nick's favorite time to play: score close, tension high, clock running low. Jamie, as usual, was skating with his stick in the air. Nick had told him a hundred times: *If your stick's in the air, I don't know where you want the pass.* When would that dickhead learn? Finally, Ramsey got the puck on a rebound and started taking it up ice, but his stickhandling left a lot to be desired.

"Dump and chase, asshole, dump and chase," Nick muttered. "Who the hell do you think you are?"

Sure enough, Tompkins intercepted and did exactly what Ramsey should have done; the Cougar forwards back-checked furiously. Ray and a Tompkins player reached the puck at once, mucked it up in a corner—and then Ray was whistled for holding.

Nick could see Griff getting nervous again. Another penalty kill, more traffic in his crease. Tompkins won the face-off and took full advantage, keeping the puck in the Cougars' zone and pounding Griff with shot after shot. He rose to the occasion—skate save, stick save, pad save— but no sooner would he get a two-second break while somebody took the puck behind the net than they were banging away at him again.

Finally, Tompkins' perseverance paid off. Griff dove, but no good. Tompkins' sticks and arms were in the air, and Griff just lay still on the ice in that way Nick knew so well—and hated so much. Finally Griff pounded his fist on the ice and heaved himself to his blades. Wasn't he embarrassed to let everybody in the building see how he felt?

The last minute was pure anticlimax, with the Tompkins fans screaming and the Shoreline fans sitting stone-faced.

When it was over, Devin said firmly, "You should go to the locker room."

"What do you care, Dev?"

"I just think you should go and be with the team."

He looked at her. If he wanted to have any hope of getting anywhere tonight, he'd better listen. Or at least pretend to.

"Yeah, I guess you're right," he admitted, standing. "Meet you in the lobby."

He moved slowly; by the time he reached the locker room, the door was shut, just as he'd planned. Now he'd hang for a while—*hide* was probably the more accurate word—then go back and tell the girls the team was showering.

Unfortunately, he'd forgotten the father factor. The

dads loitered in the locker room hall like rock groupies at the stage door, and by the time Nick heard them coming it was too late. The hallway was a dead end. He was cornered.

"—to be seventeen again, with nothing to worry about but sex and hockey." Deke's father's voice boomed against the concrete, followed by the others' laughter.

When they turned the corner, Nick saw his father among them. They all got paternal right away. "Nick!" Mr. Connelly approached him with earnest concern. "Why aren't you in there?"

Before Nick could think of a response, Mr. Connelly—self-appointed head hockey dad—had a grip on his shoulder and was opening the door to the room.

Coach Mac stopped in midsentence, turning, annoyed at the intrusion. The team, sitting solemn and sullen on the benches, all looked up.

"Sorry, Coach," Mr. Connelly said. "Heh-heh. I found this stray Renegade in the hall." He pushed Nick in and shut the door again.

"Taglio," Coach growled, "you been in this building the whole game?"

"Yeah." Nick felt himself blushing; fortunately, with his dark skin it wasn't too obvious.

"Well, tell me, hotshot—are you still part of this team, or not?"

"Yeah."

"Because if you're well enough to show up at a game, goddammit, you're well enough to sit behind the bench and support your teammates. You got that?"

"Sorry, Coach."

"And as long as you're on my roster, you come to this building dressed like a gentleman, or you stay home! Now siddown!"

Nick sat.

Coach consulted his clipboard. "Chamberlain, the general idea when passing is, there has to be somebody to pass *to*. Get it?"

Jamie nodded.

"You seem to hope somebody'll magically appear just because you've got a defenseman bearing down on you. And Ramsey, for Chrissake, dump and chase! *Dump and chase!* How the hell many times do I have to tell you?"

Nick leaned his forearms on his knees, ducking his head to hide his satisfaction.

"The object, my friend, is to get the little black rubber thing in their zone. Not to show off some fancy stick-handling you *think* you learned in hockey camp!"

Ramsey nodded.

Now Mac turned his full fury on Griff, pointing. "And you!" he roared. "I am so goddamn sick of your self-defeating antics, I could puke!"

Unlike the others, who hung their heads while Coach berated them, Griff stared right back at him.

"What is this, a day care center? You act like a toddler out there, Burroughs! Do I know when you're getting no support? Yes! Do I know when you're getting battered? Yes! Do I need your goddamn theatrics in every single game you play to show me these things? *No!*" Mac roared in Griff's face.

Nick was transfixed and terrified; Griff looked ready to attack.

Coach stepped back and addressed the entire team. "You looked like a bunch of little baby faggots out there tonight! Losers! Not because of the final score, no!" Coach made his left thumb and forefinger into an L and pushed it against Griff's forehead. "Loser for letting your emotions rule your play!" He stamped Ray, Ramsey, Jamie and everybody else within reach: "Loser for giving up . . . loser for playing dead . . . loser for that pansy-ass checking, and you!" He whirled on Nick, startling him, and planted the L right on the letter of his jacket. "You're the biggest loser of all, coming to this building and not supporting your teammates!" Then he announced: "You better all come prepared to work Monday." Translation: *I plan to make practice a living hell.* Everybody groaned. "And Taglio, if you're at school, I expect you to be there, even if you just sit on the bench and play with yourself!"

As soon as Mac stomped out, slamming the door behind him, Nick spread his legs and made the jerk-off motion. Nervous laughter filled the room.

"All *right*, Nick," said their assistant coach, who was just out of college—but he was holding back a smile himself.

"Oh yeah, I'm glad you think it's funny," Griff snapped at Nick.

"What's *your* problem?" Nick shot back.

Griff didn't answer, just pulled off his leg pads. The rest of the team was silent—watching, listening, but trying to pretend they were busy with their own pads.

"Did any of that surprise you?" Nick continued. "Was any of it new?"

Griff tugged off a skate and flung it against a metal locker. "Shut the fuck up, Nick, okay?"

Now Nick sat back with a baffled sigh, clapping a hand to his chest: *What, me?*

Griffin headed for the showers. Just before Steve followed, he leaned down to Nick and muttered, "See what I mean?"

On the ride to Jamie's house, Griff white-knuckled the steering wheel and Maddy kept sending confused looks over the back of the seat at Devin. Nick had told the girls nothing—as far as he was concerned, what went on in the room stayed in the room. You only talked about it to teammates.

Maddy reached over to rub Griff's neck; Nick was disgusted by his pathetic attempt at a smile. With what Griff was getting, he had no right to be pulling the pouty act with Maddy. A cartoon lightbulb brightened over Nick's head. Maybe he had this backward. Maybe if he was more like Griffin, all emotional and sensitive . . .

When Griff pulled up to the curb, Nick knew he and Devin should go inside first to give Griff and Maddy privacy. But right away, Griff got out and slammed the door.

"Oh my *God*," Devin said. "Nick . . ."

Maddy turned. "Yeah, Nick, what happened?"

"Ask *him*, Mad." Nick stared mysteriously out the window.

Maddy got out of the car. "We'll be there in a minute," Devin told her. "Did you guys have a fight?" she asked when Maddy was gone. "Nick?"

"I don't know what *his* problem is. *I'm* the one who—" He cut himself off.

"What?" she urged. "Tell me."

He shook his head bravely, dashed an imaginary tear from his eye. *Shameless,* he thought. *You are shameless.*

"Ohhh, *honey*," she whimpered, and swung around to sit, facing him, in his lap.

"Don't, Dev," he mumbled.

"Don't what?"

"Torment me. Not tonight." He dropped his head, fidgeting with a jacket snap.

"Is that what you think, baby? Is that what I do?" she asked, stroking his face.

"No . . . not on purpose, but—" He gave her his gamer smile. "Never mind. Just . . . not tonight, okay?"

"Okay," she whispered as her hands moved down,

tugging at his fly. She started to kiss him; he pretended to resist, then give in. Now, to his complete shock, she was wriggling down between his legs, her head in his lap.

"Dev . . . no." The protest was phony, but the croak in his voice was real.

"Yes," she said.

# 12

At first, he was a new man. He trailed her around like a puppy, holding her hand, staring into her eyes, fetching her Corona ponies until she whispered, "Oh my *God*, I should've done that a long time ago!"

But when she'd had enough she playfully pushed him away, giggling: "Nii-*iick*! You're smothering me! Go play with your little friends."

So he went to the family room, where they were re-hashing the game and trashing Mac, drinking soda and beer, the music turned up loud. Jamie's parents didn't ex-actly sanction drinking; they just sort of looked the other way. And the other parents didn't exactly sanction Jamie's parents looking the other way; they just sort of looked the other way from them looking the other way, jokily asking each other and the Chamberlains why the kids always wanted to hang out at Jamie's.

Griff was pretty well out of his funk now that he had a couple of beers in him. He and Nick acted like nothing had happened. Girls had to have a big, emotional crisis, complete with heartfelt apologies. Guys just started talking again.

As they all went on and on about who should have done what on the ice, Nick's thoughts drifted back out to the car. . . . Incredible. It just didn't seem possible that she had finally done it, or that anything could feel that good. And he only felt a little guilty about getting it under more or less false pretenses.

But it wasn't as though he didn't love her. He did. And it wasn't as though he'd given her an ultimatum or anything, as Deke had suggested Thursday in the caf. Deke had heard of his dilemma, so of course the senior sex god had to give his esteemed opinion: *Dump her, Tag. There's a hundred girls in this school who'd jump at the chance to do you.*

All at once he could hear Deke's father saying, *Nothing to worry about but sex and hockey.* And here they were. Nick almost laughed out loud.

But parents were so full of it—what were kids supposed to be worried about? Crushing al-Qaeda? Brokering peace between Israel and Palestine? Solving global warming?

When the parents were kids, how had they spent *their* time? Adults were always talking about how kids just aren't *kids* anymore . . . they grow up so *fast* nowadays . . . blah blah blah. But did they ever stop to wonder why? Did they ever think maybe it was because the adults were always putting their problems on kids?

Every time you turned around somebody was making you sign up to serve soup to the homeless or take a walk for some gruesome illness. Collect soap for Guatemala, diapers for Afghanistan, money for the 9/11 families.

In social studies, they were always having to talk about hate crimes and terrorism and gun control and drug abuse and AIDS. Did the adults have all this to deal with when they were in high school?

But now kids were supposed to spend all their time worrying about the problems the parents' generation had created—and was too lazy to fix.

"Nick. Nick."

"Huh?" He looked up at Griff. Somebody's cell was ringing. His. Now who could *that* possibly be? He got up and went into the bathroom. "Yeah."

"Hi, it's Mom."

"Really?"

"Where are you?"

"At Jamie's. Just like I said. Hey, I'm gonna sleep at Griff's, okay?"

"No, you are not. You are sleeping at home."

"Why?"

"Nick, don't push your luck, all right?"

"Just tell me why."

"Nick . . ."

"Because you don't trust me? What do you think I'm gonna do? I'll be there at midnight. Call me at midnight."

"Oh, okay—I'll call you and you'll say, 'I'm there!' and how will I know where you really are?"

"Call me on *their* phone!"

The phone changed hands. "Nick," the wop said, "be home by midnight." Then he hung up.

Now Nick was determined to stay out past curfew. But in the next half hour, his head started killing him, and he got really sleepy. So: Go home, and climb into his nice, comfortable bed? And let his parents think they'd scared him? Or stay here, and be miserable?

After a while he realized the decision was bigger than him. He had to get off his feet. Maybe he'd just go and lie down in Griff's car.

Oh, screw pride. He wanted to be home.

Quietly he asked Griff to drive him; then he went to tell Devin. But before he reached the living room doorway, he stopped short.

Ramsey.

What was Ramsey doing here, and why was Devin prancing before him, shifting from tiptoe to tiptoe, talking like she had the world's most exciting news? They were laughing. She was holding a beer. She pushed her hair back with thumb and forefinger, tossing her head. She didn't see Nick, who quickly walked away.

"She's gonna stay," Nick told Griff. "You'll take her home later, right?"

"Sure."

Nick slumped down on the car seat, pressing a cold palm to his forehead.

"You felt okay earlier?" Griff asked.

He nodded.

"Nick, I hate to say it, but—you were a little, like, File Not Found before."

Nick didn't answer.

"It's weird—you were totally yourself, and then you just . . ." Griff passed a hand in front of his own face.

"Thanks," Nick said. "I'll be sure to report this to my neurologist."

Nick's cell rang. He ignored it.

"That's you," Griff said.

"You're kidding."

The cell finally stopped.

"That's Devin," Griff said. "You didn't tell her you were leaving."

Nick looked out the window. The cell started up again.

"Nick—for Chrissake!" Griff exploded.

Nick hit *Send*. "Yeah."

"Where *are* you?" Devin asked. "Somebody just said you left."

"Somebody was right."

"Are you okay? Why didn't you tell me?"

"You were busy."

A silence, then: "Oh my *God*, Nick. I'm not supposed to *talk* to people?"

He didn't answer.

"You're *so* ridiculous. How could . . . oh my *God*, Nick. He *has* a girlfriend!"

"Oh, really? Where was she?"

"I don't know, I—"

"And so what if he has a girlfriend?" Nick interrupted. "Guys with girlfriends never hit on other girls?"

"I don't have to take this," she said icily, and hung up.

But he couldn't let Griff know that, so he said into the phone: "This conversation is over," and hit *End*.

Griff gave his deep sigh of concern. As they turned into the driveway, Nick pulled the seat belt over himself: ten to one, his mother would be peeking out the second she heard the car. But no. He released the belt and opened the door. "Thanks."

"No problem, dude," Griff said.

Nick was depressed by the sad, sympathetic tone.

He turned his key in the lock; the kitchen was dark and cold. But in the living room, his parents were cozy enough, huddled together under a quilt, a bowl of popcorn in their laps.

"Hey," Nick said, standing in the doorway.

His father paused the tape. "Hey, Nick."

"Are you all right?" his mother asked.

"Yeah . . . yeah, I just . . ." He shrugged. "I'm tired. So, no use 'biting off your nose to spite your face,'" he said, quoting them with his fingers.

They actually laughed.

"What're you watching?" He turned his attention to the frozen screen.

"It's called *Best in Show,*" his mom said. "It's pretty funny."

"You want to watch with us for a while?" his father asked.

"Thanks, but . . . I think I'll go to bed." His cell rang; he stepped back into the kitchen to answer. "Yeah?"

"I just want to say one thing, okay?" She was crying.

"Okay." He went outside. "Where are you?"

"I'm home, all right? And I hope you're happy for humiliating me, and—"

"Humiliating *you*!" he protested. "How did *I* humiliate *you*?" He walked off the porch and started pacing the snowy yard.

"Oh, what, Nick, I humiliated you because I dared to talk to Cade? Screw that, Nick!" She was sobbing so hard he could barely understand her. "No, *you* humiliated *me*. Everybody's like, 'Nick just left, you know,' and I'm all, 'He left? What?' " She caught her breath with a gasp, swallowed. "And what I want to say, what I just don't get, is how you could, how could you treat me that way after what happened tonight?"

"Dev." He was shivering, shaking with cold and . . . whatever else.

"Because you say you love me, and I was so happy, I felt so close to you after that, and then you go and turn on me? What is that, Nick? What *is* that?" She covered the phone, but he could still hear the muffled sobs.

"Dev . . . I'm sorry. I'm sorry. You listening? It's just, I love you so much, I do, and—" Forget his phony act in the car. Now he really *did* feel like crying. How could he have totally wrecked this night? His jaw was aching, his head breaking. He kept his free hand in his jacket pocket and his head bent to the phone. Snow fell into his shoes. "You there? Dev?"

"Yeah," she choked out.

"It was so incredible, I just, I don't know, I loved you even more, and that made me even more jealous. You know?"

She seemed to be calming down.

"I'm an asshole," he admitted. "You *know* I am. Did I ever pretend not to be an asshole?"

She laughed, a little, through her tears.

"I'm sorry. It won't happen again, I swear to God."

A worried little leprechaun opened the kitchen door and called, "Nick?"

He held up his index finger; she shut the door.

"Where are you?" Devin asked.

"Outside."

She sniffled. "You should go in."

"Will you pick me up tomorrow?"

"Yeah." It was their standing Sunday morning date: her mother dropped them at confirmation class at nine, then they went to Mass, then out to breakfast.

"Okay. Love you, Dev."

"Me too."

Back inside, he took three Tylenol.

"Everything okay?" his mom asked when he walked through the living room.

"Yeah."

His teeth chattered as he changed into flannel pants, old Rangers sweatshirt, dry socks. He would make this up to Devin. Keep his promise not to do it again, for starters. And tomorrow, or next time they were alone together, he wouldn't even mention sex. Just hold her and kiss her. . . . God, why did his parents keep the house so cold?

The sounds of their movie and their laughter comforted

him, like when he was a little kid falling asleep upstairs and he'd hear his mother humming as she put clean towels in the linen closet.

And then for some reason, he felt like being with them. He picked up his pillow and down quilt and went back into the living room. "Think I *will* watch with you awhile."

"Want to lie here, buddy?" his dad asked, moving to get up from the big couch.

"No, no . . ." Nick tossed his pillow on the little couch. "This is good." He scrunched up, pulling the quilt to his chin.

A perfect young couple were screaming at each other, frantically trying to find their dog's toy, Busy Bee. Nick's parents were laughing.

He smiled, and closed his eyes, and slept.

# 13

Better? Worse? The same?

Nick examined his pupils in every mirror he passed. He tried not to be "unusually combative," and even kept his mouth shut in Diversity Workshop, when the exercise was "The Advantages of Being a White Male" and the whole class was glancing at him, waiting for a laugh. He did neuro drills on himself—he was pretty sure he was definitely starting to get better.

Except for the headaches. And the fog.

When he tried to do his homework, he just could not concentrate. But which part of his brain was at fault? The part that was injured, or the part that couldn't stop thinking about what he'd hear at clinic Wednesday?

He tried to look alert whenever he was around his parents—that alone tired him out. And school . . . by the time he turned up at practice on Monday, he was beat. He sat on the bench, shivering, watching the team do suicide sprints and crawls across the ice. Finally Mac came over, patted his shoulder and told him to go home.

Nick stopped at the Rite-Aid and bought his own bottle of extra-strength Tylenol with his Christmas money, because he didn't want his mother to know how much he was using. He came home to an empty house, fell right to sleep—and woke with a jolt at six-thirty.

Brian was alone in the kitchen, taking a bowl of Easy Mac from the microwave. "Hey," he said.

Nick lifted his shoulders, turned up his palms.

"Tractor-trailer overturned on Ninety-one. She's in that one." He poured the powdery cheese over the macaroni and stirred it up. "Accident on the Z. He's in that one. I'm like Shadow Traffic over here." He raised an imaginary phone to each ear.

Nick smiled and sat on a stool at the kitchen bar.

"You feel okay?"

"Yeah." The truth was, he felt a little dizzy, though the headache was gone. But after the other night, he wasn't about to give Gallant the details.

Brian sat beside him. "It must be so freaky, waiting for Wednesday, finding out what he's gonna say. . . . Sort of a Damocles hanging over your head."

Nick perked right up: got him! "A what?" he repeated casually.

"You know. Sort of like a Damocles."

"*The* sword *of* Damocles, Einstein," Nick informed him. He shook his head, snickering: "Sort of like a Damocles."

Blood colored Brian's Irish skin. "Well, what's a sword of Damocles?"

"Damocles was this Greek myth guy," Nick explained. "His boss was really rich, and Damocles was like, 'Dude, you're so lucky!' " Nick gave Damocles a stoned skateboarder voice; Brian grinned. "So his boss goes, 'Oh, you think so? You want to try my life?' And Damocles is all: 'No duh!' So he's sitting at this incredible banquet table, unbelievable food everywhere, blazing hot girls waiting on him, and he's like, 'Dude, what're you talking about? This is the tits!' But then all of a sudden he catches this flash on his plate, this sort of shadow. And he looks up and there's a friggin' sword hanging over his head, by like a thread!"

Brian was listening intently, solemnly chewing his Easy Mac.

"And Damocles is like, 'Whoa, boss, dude! What's up with *this* shit?' And his boss says, 'Well, yeah, this is the way I live, dog.'"

After a pause, Brian said, "Yeah, go on . . ."

Nick shrugged. "That's it. I think the point is, no matter how rich you are or how lucky you seem, you could have it all taken away at any time." Realizing the significance of his words, he looked away fast.

"Wow," Brian said, staring at him in wonder. "That's amazing! I said 'Damocles' without even knowing the story, and . . . you're *him*, Nick."

"Cosmic," Nick mumbled. "Is there any more Easy Mac?"

Skating, all alone, on a rink much bigger than in real life. Skating hard, head down, the puck on his tape, and there's open ice, nobody between him and the goalie. But as he positions himself to take the shot, he sees it in the corner of his eye—the glint of steel, too late to square up . . .

Gasping for breath, Nick awakened sitting straight up in bed. His T-shirt, his neck, his hair were damp with sweat.

Clinic day.

He felt like a condemned prisoner as he dragged himself to the shower, then got dressed.

As Brian was leaving for school, Nick desperately

wanted to say, *Don't go, stay here,* because as long as Brian stayed, the day would not have to move forward.

In the car he was quiet. He didn't dare to hope, and he couldn't bear not to.

When they got beyond Blakeman's waiting room, the big man and his puppy greeted them—and separated Nick from his parents just like on cop shows when the kid's about to be arrested.

"Why don't you folks come with me," Blakeman said. "Nick, Dr. Wu is going to examine you, and then you'll join us."

He was too stunned to respond. Blakeman didn't want to shine lights in his eyes or thump on his head? There was no doubt now. . . .

Nick turned back like a panicked little kid, as if his parents could save him from this. As if they would.

During the examination, he was totally numb—too scared for sarcasm, too desperate for questions. If he asked anything, Wu might dash the last ember of hope that still glowed in his brain.

Finally, Wu ushered him to Blakeman's office and opened the door.

Three heads turned. His parents gave their special, let's-be-brave smiles.

"Ah!" Blakeman said, and that one short sound held everything Nick needed to know.

Sound the horn.

Power up the Zamboni.

It's over.

# SECOND

Nick stood still and tense in the doorway, with the adrenaline rush of waiting for the puck to drop. The question was no longer what they were going to say, but how he would react. He knew he'd lose the face-off—but where would he be skating to next?

The wop slipped into take-charge-dad mode. "Nick," he said with a kindly smile. "Sit down."

"No." Nick leaned against the wall. "Say what you have to say, so I can get out of here."

Blakeman said it: "I cannot in good conscience clear you to play hockey again."

"Yeah, right *now*. I know I'm not ready to go back *yet*, but—"

"I can't, Nick. We've discussed this."

"There's gotta be . . . isn't there some sort of rehab I can do?"

"Yes, it's called cognitive rehabilitation. We'll get to that in a minute. But it's separate from what we're talking about now."

Nick started rocking back and forth. "Meaning?"

"Your going through rehab won't change my mind about hockey."

"Next year," Nick said. "I'll be fine by September, right?"

"Nick, understand this," Blakeman said, trying to be gentle. "It's not a question of when you'll feel better or be fully recovered. It's a question of what happens next time, and the time after that. We talked about this. Each concussion—"

"I'll change my game," Nick interrupted. "Learn to keep my head up. I'll become more of a finesse player. I can do it."

"But it's not entirely up to you," Blakeman said. "It's not as though if you do x, y and z, you'll never get hit again."

Nick turned to his parents. "Second opinion," he said, hearing the desperation in his voice. "Who's he, God? Can we just get a second opinion?"

His mother avoided his eyes. And his father said: "We already got a second opinion, Nick."

Lying. He was lying.

"Yesterday. Mom and I went up to Farmington. To UConn. We brought your pictures. Dr. Blakeman faxed your files. The doctor's one of the top pediatric sports guys in the country, Nick. He backed up Dr. Blakeman right down the line."

"I've gone over it again and again," Blakeman said. "I've consulted with a number of colleagues." He rattled off various head problems with an alphabet of abbreviations, then finished with: "At this point, your neurologic function *is* compromised. And the cumulative, long-term effects of this type of injury can be devastating—Muhammad Ali, for instance. Nick, I do not think you should play again."

Nick turned to his parents. "He's wrong. I'll be okay. You can't do this."

"Nick, if we let you play and something happened to you . . . we couldn't live with ourselves," his father said.

"Well, you won't be able to live with *me* if you don't let me play," Nick said.

"Oh, you're threatening us now?"

His mother broke in: "Honey, this was not an easy decision. We know how important hockey is to you."

"No." Nick shook his head. "Obviously, you don't." Then he addressed Blakeman: "See, you don't get it. I might've been able to go to college off this. Ask them." He waved a hand at his parents. "Ask them what the Quinnipiac coach said to them last year when he saw me in the all-star game."

"Nick, you're a very bright kid. You can go to college off *this*." Blakeman tapped his own skull. "But a couple more concussions, and you might not go to college at all."

Nick folded his arms and stared at the floor.

"There are other sports you can participate in," Blakeman dared to say. "Noncontact sports."

Nick looked up. "Like what? Track? Go run around in circles in my little shorts? Or should I buy a couple of Speedo suits and take up swimming? What else is there? What? You tell me."

His mother was bouncing her knee up and down, twisting the rings on her finger.

"Well, there are other ways you can stay involved in hockey," Blakeman said. "Coaching children, maybe."

"Hey, I know!" Nick said. "Let's call it community service! I can be like the guy in *The Mighty Ducks*!"

"What about reffing?" Blakeman offered.

"Yeah. I'll become one of those jerks I've hated for ten years. That's good, that'll fix everything."

"Nick," his father mumbled.

"What, am I embarrassing you? Aw, gosh, I'm *so* sorry. But guess what? I don't give a shit!"

"Nicholas!" his mother said.

"You people sit here, all calm and reasonable, and just take my whole fuckin' life away from me, and I'm supposed to, what, be polite about it? Oh, thank you *so* much for your time, Dr. Blakeman." He pushed himself away from the wall. "Good day."

"Nicky . . . ," his mom called.

"Give him a minute," Blakeman said.

Nick walked down the hall, past the nurses' station, out of the office, into the corridor.

And then he started to run.

He had no idea where he was going; this hospital was like a maze. He knew he had to go down to get outside, so he kept running, blindly, until an exit sign led him to a set of stairs.

Down three flights, through the busy main lobby, and out. He would just run around the block, he thought. Run so that he wouldn't break down and cry.

But the block wasn't a block, and before long he was lost in the tangle of the medical complex. His wind was spent, and when he stopped to breathe, to locate himself, he realized he had no idea where he was.

He looked up at the identical high buildings. Which one was Blakeman's? The fog was bearing down. The world whirled around him. *Calm down*, he told himself.

*Figure it out. You're not three years old.*

But that was exactly what he felt like—a lost kid, not

knowing where to turn. He began to walk, slowly, carefully. With each step, his legs quivered. Could he ask somebody? Ask what? *Do you know where Dr. Blakeman's office is?* He stuffed his hands in his pockets. His cell. Of course. But what was he going to do, call his parents on their cell? *It's Nicky. I'm lost.*

No, he would figure this out. But first . . .

He sat on a bench and leaned over, arms on his knees. So dizzy. *That* would be cool, to keel over right in the medical complex courtyard. After the last concussion, he'd done it in Spanish class. Slithered out of his chair and landed in a heap, they said. He'd never been more embarrassed than when he came to with the school nurse holding smelling salts under his nose like he was some British girl in a gown, and Señora Silva standing there looking terrified while Jamie and a football player hauled him to his feet as the rest of the class muttered and giggled nervously.

His father had rushed to pick him up, called Blakeman . . . and that was the first day the dreaded words had been spoken: *postconcussion syndrome.*

After a while Nick straightened up and took a look around. Find the parking garage. Be at the car, waiting, by the time they got there. How hard could that be?

He started walking again, aimlessly. A weird sort of panic crept through him. This was ridiculous. Why couldn't he figure it out? Was his brain that far gone?

Or maybe he couldn't find his way on his own because every time he was here, he was trailing after his parents. That was it. Definitely. The place was confusing even to them. He could hear them saying to each other: *Do we get on the purple elevators or follow the orange signs?* as Nick stood behind them, rolling his eyes.

Then all at once, he was saved. Here was Nurse

Janeece, walking right toward him. At least he thought it was her. She had a knitted cap pulled down over her ears, but as he grew closer he knew her face, her confident walk. She'd be able to help him.

She seemed to look right at him, but just as Nick was about to speak, she shifted her eyes and continued on.

Nick flattened himself against the brick wall as if she'd shoved him against it. *Faced, Taglio*, he thought, pushing out his breath in a noiseless laugh, shaking his head. In the hospital she was always good to him—not sappy and sweet, but caring, in her tough way. So why would she treat him like this now? As he watched her step briskly along the sidewalk, disappearing into the crowd, he understood: she hadn't ignored him, she just hadn't seen him. Today, he was not her job.

Just part of the boy wallpaper.

Finally, by sheer chance, he found the garage. But where were they parked? He stood at the elevator and looked at the little symbols. They were on the Charter Oak level. Definitely . . . or was it Nutmeg? He took the elevator to Nutmeg and started walking. No Cavalier. Then he turned to go up to Charter Oak, and there it was—with his parents in it.

Relief washed over him. But when his father got out and opened the back door on his side, Nick walked around to the passenger's side instead. Neither parent told him to put on his seat belt.

At least getting lost had stopped him from thinking about hockey for a while. Now it all came back, like when you wake up in the morning feeling all right until you remember what left you in a bad mood when you went to bed.

About five minutes into the drive, his cell rang. The

dashboard clock read 11:40. Lunchtime at school. Devin. Nick switched off the power and put on his headphones, skipping ahead to find "Where Are You Going?" Dave sang about being no superman, having no answers:

*I am no hero, oh, that's for sure . . .*

Nick turned the music up loud and shut his eyes.

When his parents tried to drop him off at school, Nick said, "I'm not going." Without a word, they took him home.

He got an ice pack from the freezer and went to his room. Everything was about hockey, from the sticks in the corner to the frames on the wall. The *SI* and *Hockey Illustrated* covers of Lindros and Gretzky. The *Hockey News* and *Hockey Night in Boston* magazines. The needlework his aunt Michelle had given him: *You miss 100 percent of the shots you don't take—Wayne Gretzky.* On his dresser was a statue of Jesus playing hockey with two little boys, a joke birthday present from Griff. Next to that stood Starting Lineup figures of Lindros, Gretzky and Gordie Howe.

His very first pair of hockey skates hung from a hook on the wall. They were so tiny, yet he could still remember wearing them. Still recall stepping onto the ice with a stick for the first time and realizing that he was going to love this game . . .

His new stick, an Easton one-piece Synergy, stood in the corner. He picked it up. Lying on the bed, he draped the ice pack over his forehead and twirled the stick in his hands. The newest, some said the best, stick you could buy, made of graphite, Kevlar and carbon. He had wanted it so bad, but his parents had sworn he wasn't getting a $150 stick—not the way *he* went through sticks. But then he'd had the grade-three, the result of a brutal, but accidental, collision in a scrimmage. A week later, the Synergy had turned up beside his birthday cake.

How had it gotten home from the Quebec game? Who had carried it off the ice for him, collected his helmet, his gloves?

Next thing he knew, the phone was ringing and the stick was across his chest. He wandered to the kitchen, listening for the machine to pick up.

"Hi!" the wop said cheerfully. "Please leave a message for Mike, Kathy, Nick or Brian, and we'll get back to you as soon as we can!"

Beep!

"Nick?" Devin said. "I'm trying your cell all afternoon. Where are you? I'm—"

He picked up. "Hey."

"Hi!" she said breathlessly. "Where've you been, how'd it go?"

"Um . . . it's over."

She gave an exaggerated, dramatic sigh. "Thank *God*. When can you play?"

Nick let the pause linger, aching for her misunderstanding to be the reality.

"Nicky?"

"No," he said. "I *can't* play."

"What do you mean?"

Right off the hop she was on his nerves, with this little defiant edge to her voice—as if he was telling her *she* couldn't do something. She'd known this was a possibility. She'd known since last time.

"I mean, I'm finished. I can't play again."

"Ever?"

"Generally, that's the meaning of the word *finished*."

"Well—oh my *God*, what did they say? What did *you* say? I mean, didn't you *say* anything?"

"I said plenty, Devin. But they're like, 'Me parent, you kid, end of story.' "

"You can't let them do this to you!" She sounded panicked. "You have to fight them, Nick. I mean, hockey, it's like—it's your whole life!"

"Yeah, I tried that argument. They say, 'Well, unless you want to end up like Muhammad Ali, you have to quit.' "

"That's bullshit!" she snapped. "Oh my God, that is so *stupid*! By the time you're Ali's age, they'll have ways to fix stuff like that!"

"Dev, this is not helping. Can you come over?"

Tick, tick . . . "Um, no, I can't. My parents are on a jihad. They want me home after school to watch Brat Boy."

"Whatever."

"But Nick—you're gonna fight this. Aren't you?"

"I don't know, I—"

"I mean, oh my God, it's the middle of the season, and you guys could actually get to the playoffs this year. *How* can they make you stop playing?"

"Blakeman said my neurologic function is quote compromised at this point. Compromised, Dev—that's not good."

"But you'll get better. So, okay, maybe *not* this season. But next, right? Can't you get that much out of them?"

"Devin, go look up *never* in the dictionary."

"You don't have to get snotty with me, Nick," she said coldly.

"You keep hammering away. I kind of feel like shit about this, Dev, you know?"

"I can't believe you're just gonna cave! That is so *not you*!"

He abandoned all hope of understanding. Wasn't this a perfect end to the day? But maybe she was right. Maybe he *was* giving up too easily.

"At least think about it, okay?" Now she was using her sexy, breathy voice. "I mean—it's you I'm thinking about, sweetie. I just don't see you living without hockey."

"Yeah."

"Just humor them for a couple of days. Then, you know, tell them."

He didn't answer.

"Here's my bus. I have to go, boo." After she clicked off, he paced the house. Then he called her back. "The cellular customer you are trying to reach is on the phone," the cyber-operator told him. "Please leave a message and—"

Nick put the phone down. He stared out the living room window, cooling his forehead on the glass.

# 15

His cell started ringing as soon as he turned it back on.

"Yeah?" he said.

"Hey," Griff answered.

"I'm done."

"I know."

"How?"

"Your mother called mine, and mine called me."

Nick shook his head, twisting his mouth into a grim grin. The hockey mom grapevine. That was one thing he wouldn't miss. "You tell everybody?" he asked.

"No! Course not. Listen—I'm coming to pick you up."

"Okay."

At Black Rock Fort they sat in the car, looking out at the harbor. Nick told Griff the Blakeman story as near as he could remember it, though he left out the parts that made him look like a fruitcake.

"Ah, this bites," Griff said when he finished.

"Yeah."

"We were gonna be captains together." It wasn't just brag. As the only two picked for varsity freshman year, they were a sure thing for cocaptains as seniors.

"Yeah, and Devin's giving me all this shit. 'Why aren't you fighting them, you can't give in so easy.'"

"Really?"

Nick nodded. "She doesn't get it. I mean, I tried every angle. Blakeman's like, 'The MTBI of the PCS of the SIS of the RHI of the ZXCVB,'" Nick recited in a lofty voice. "How do you compete with that? 'But, dude, I really really really want to skate.'"

Griff snickered.

"How was practice?"

"All right."

"You think Mac knows?"

"He didn't say anything. But he didn't mention you, either."

Nick stared across the water at the lights of New Haven.

"You want to get a burger?" Griff asked. "I'm buying."

"You're buying? Be fairly warned—I haven't eaten anything since breakfast."

"Uh-oh." Griff took out his cell and speed-dialed. "Call your mom," he told Nick, then said into the phone: "Hi. You home yet? . . . Oh. Well, I'm gonna eat with Nick, okay? . . . Yeah. I will. See you." He looked at Nick. "My mom sends her love."

Nick nodded.

"Did you leave a note when you left?"

"Note," Nick scoffed. "Notes are for faggots like you, Mule."

"Then call her."

"Screw that. Let 'em wonder."

Griff made a show of tugging at the gearshift, grunting dramatically. "Oh, I forgot. This car won't move till every-body's called their mom."

Nick laughed through his nose, shook his head, pulled his cell from his pocket.

"God, you're such a woman," he said.

When Nick got back home, his family was sitting around the living room like it was a funeral parlor and the corpse had just arrived. Brian looked so miserable, Nick yanked his hair as he passed the couch.

"Coach called," his father said.

"You tell him?"

"I told him earlier. He was calling for you. He said he'd call back."

Nick kept walking toward his room.

"Nick," his mother said. "Can we talk?"

"About what?"

"Your rehab, for one thing."

"No hockey, no rehab," Nick answered, and shut his door. He called Mac right away. "Hi, Coach. It's Nick."

"*Hey,* buddy."

Nick didn't feel like hearing heartfelt voices. *Let's just get this over with.* "Hi, yeah, my parents said you called, so—"

"Yeah, Nicky, I talked to your dad this afternoon. He gave me the bad news."

"Yep, well, you know—I don't agree with it, but I don't get a vote."

"Nick, the most important thing is your health. So what the doctors say, that's gotta be the final word, right?"

"I guess."

"But, Nick, I just wanted to say . . . I'll really miss you on the team. Not only your playing, but—your presence. I mean, you've always got a good attitude, on the ice and off. You got a ton of heart, Nicky, and you know I was expecting great things from you."

"Uh-huh."

"You've heard me say it, if you'd been as good in bantams as you were last year, one of the prep schools would have picked you up."

Nick sat on the edge of the bed, holding his breath. *Are we done here?*

"I appreciated you giving a hundred and ten percent every practice, every game, and your way with the other guys—especially Griff. And hell, with you gone, who's gonna break the tension by making fun of me behind my back?"

Nick laughed—or tried to.

"Well, I'll let you go, Nick. I know this is a difficult time. But I just want to say, as far as I'm concerned, you'll always be a Cougar. You're always welcome on that bench and in that room, and if you ever just want to come down and skate with the guys, if that's something you'd ever feel like doing . . ." His voice trailed away.

"Thanks, Coach. Thanks for everything and, um . . ." He couldn't go on.

"Okay, Nicky. You take care."

"Thanks." Nick turned off the phone. Slowly, carefully, he took his homework from his backpack, arranging it neatly on his desk in subject piles.

And piles they were; he'd done almost nothing since the concussion. He sat down and tried to conjugate Spanish verbs, but he heard Coach say, *I was expecting great things from you.* . . . He wrote a couple of Spanish sentences with vocabulary words, but his eyes started aching. Geometry, biology . . . he opened each book, stared and shut it again. *I appreciated you giving a hundred and ten percent every practice, every game. . . .* Social studies. Dyer had to be kidding with this assignment:

> Devise a project that shows how diversity affects your everyday life. This can be a written or oral project, something done on the computer, artwork or any other medium. Be creative! Feel free to discuss your project with me! What I'm looking for in this final project for Diversity Workshop is a true understanding of how diversity comes into play in America each and every day.

Well, at least he didn't have to hand it in for a few weeks. A couple of days before it was due, he'd pull something off the Internet.

*The Old Man and the Sea.* Okay. Lucas had said it was good. Maybe reading would distract him. He lay on his bed, holding the book over his head.

> He was an old man who fished alone in a skiff in the Gulf Stream and he had gone eighty-four days now without taking a fish.

*I'll really miss you on the team. Not just your playing but your presence . . .*

> He was an old man who fished alone in a skiff in the Gulf Stream and he . . .

*You're always welcome on that bench and in that room. . . .*
Nick flung the book across the room; it splatted against the wall. He took one of his old sticks from the corner and

swung it mightily against the open closet door, cracking the stick in two. Then he sank down into the desk chair, clutching his aching head.

He would never go back—not to the rink, not to the room.

He didn't want to be welcome.

He wanted to belong.

Before first period on Thursday, everything seemed normal. But by lunchtime, everybody he knew was staring at him in the halls. Guys muttered to each other; girls whispered. Teachers were nice to him.

The word was out: brain-damaged Nick had to quit hockey.

In the caf, he slid his tray onto the team's table, suddenly realizing that they were the only friends he had. Over the years, as he'd become more and more involved with hockey, his childhood friends had drifted away. Now he always ate with the team, and went to sit with Devin and Alyssa and their friends afterward.

"So, you all know, right?" Nick asked, shaking a container of chocolate milk.

"Yeah—it really sucks, Tag," Ray said.

"How can they do that to you?" Jamie asked. "I'd probably kill my parents if they made me quit hockey."

"You're a tough guy," Nick muttered.

"Yeah, Chamberlain, shut the fuck up," Steve advised.

Deke and Zach came over, slapping Nick's shoulder, grabbing him by the neck.

"Hey, Tag."

"This blows, dude."

"Yeah, I know."

Griff sat down a few seats away. He and Nick nodded to each other.

"There's no way out?" Zach asked.

"Unless I join the witness protection program," Nick said, and they all laughed.

Now Ramsey was there, offering his hand. "Nick. I'm really sorry."

"Yeah, me too," Nick said, wondering if Ramsey had found out about his jealous fit the other night. As he shook Ramsey's hand, he hoped Devin was watching.

"It's a big loss for the team," Ramsey continued.

"You guys'll do fine," Nick said.

Ramsey a Renegade. What a joke.

"Hey, Tag—can't you, like, sign one of those emancipation proclamations?" Jamie offered.

Everyone turned to Jamie, and Steve said what they were all thinking: "What are you talking about, asshole?"

"You know, like that singer did, what's-her-name, to get free from her parents?"

Nick knew exactly what he meant, but he couldn't come up with the phrase. It had to be Ramsey who said, "You mean emancipated-minor status."

"Yeah, yeah—that," Jamie agreed.

"I think you need a lot of money to get that," Ray said.

In the air, Nick drew a circle with a slash through it. They laughed.

"And a reason the judge will feel sorry for. It's always

rich kids whose parents are trying to take their money," Griff added.

"Yeah, I could just see Tag going before the judge," Steve said. "Please, your honor, it's terrible! Just because I had—" He asked Nick, aside: "How many concussions?"

"Four," Nick said.

"Just because I had four concussions, and my brain's fusilli, my wicked parents won't let me play hockey anymore."

Griff played the judge: "Four concussions! Arrest those parents for letting him play *this* long! Social worker, place that lad in the custody of the proper authorities!"

"Your honor, there's a fine Catholic facility where he'll be in the care of kind priests," Ray said, doing the social worker.

"No! No!" Nick protested, shielding himself with his arms. "Not the priests! Anything but the priests!"

When the laughter died down, they all ate in silence until Steve said, "Anyway, Tag, it sucks."

"Yeah," Jamie said, and the others muttered agreement.

Nick picked stale bread from his Italian sub. "These things are like concrete," he mumbled.

# 17

He felt like his skull was being continually crushed in a vise. He couldn't think, concentrate or even see straight some of the time, but he worked hard to hide everything, to act normal. At lunch Friday, his friends told him Mac had announced he was retiring the Renegade name, saying, "We can't have the Renegades without Taglio." They were trying to cheer him up, but it made him more miserable than ever.

To cap it all, Gallant was really getting on his nerves. Being so nice to Nick, practically tiptoeing around him, never bugging him to get off the computer, doing all his chores. And on Saturday, Brian was in and out of the house all day, friends, basketball game, friends. Brian and his little crew traveled in a pack, their mother said. Parents, Nick noticed, loved to talk about how "kids these days travel in a pack." Now the pack's laughter howled through the den walls while Nick sat at his desk, trying to catch up on schoolwork.

Every ten minutes, he'd hear the stupid jingle of Brian's cell. The middle of January, and Brian still had his ringer set to "O Christmas Tree."

Gabriel's cartoons were blaring on the living room TV.

And Devin hadn't called all day.

Nick tried putting on his headphones, but for some reason that was even worse. He felt like he needed total silence—then he'd be able to get something done. But if he went and told Brian to pipe down, his friends would be looking at Nick, feeling sorry for him and acting weird. Nick had had enough of that in school the last two days.

There was a knock at his door.

"Yeah?" he practically snarled.

His mother poked her little mick face in. "Can I get you a sandwich, Nick?"

"I'm not hungry. What you *can* do is tell your son and his minions to keep it down. And what's Gabriel having, a Nickelodeon dance party?"

"It's not that loud, honey." The sad, patronizing tone aggravated him. Then she gave him a weak smile. "Times like this, you probably regret moving down here."

*Times like this never happened before.*

"Let me figure something out," she said, and shut the door.

Five minutes later, she was back with an electric fan.

"What's that for?"

"White noise. Try it."

"Great. White noise blowing cold air on me. It's already freezing in here. Why do you people have to keep this house so cold?"

She busied herself setting the fan on his dresser, kneeling to plug it in. "There. You won't even feel it from here. See if that helps."

"Whatever," he muttered, propping his forehead in his hand, and she left again.

But it did help, and he was actually able to get some Spanish done. Later, his cell rang; he was disappointed to hear Steve's voice. Before every game, the parents took turns hosting dinner for the team. Tonight was the Genoveses' turn, and Steve wanted to make sure Nick was coming.

"Nah," Nick said. "I, um, I got a lot of school shit to catch up on."

"Tag." Steve made the name into a statement. "*You're* missing the hockey dinner to stay home and do school shit?"

"Well, I just—" *I just don't see the point of going to the dinners when I'm not on the team.* "It's gotta get done. But thanks."

"But you're coming to the game, right?"

"Um . . . I don't know."

"Dude. Come on. You're not gonna bail on us, are you?"

"I'll have to see how much I get done," Nick lied. As soon as he hung up, he worked up his nerve and called Devin.

"Hi," she said. "I can't talk long, I'm waiting to get my hair cut."

"I was just wondering what you want to do tonight."

A little pause. "Aren't we going to Jamie's?"

"I mean before that. You want to see a movie?"

"A *movie*? I'm going to the game. Aren't you?"

Nick stared at the wall and let out his breath very slowly.

"Nick?"

"No."

"How come?"

"I just don't feel like it."

"Well, *I'm* going to the game."

"Yeah, you made that clear. Now just add 'So fuck you, Nick.' "

"Okay then, fuck you, Nick," she answered, and clicked off.

He should have known better than to call her bluff. In fact, he *did* know better.

But he was getting sick of her queen bitch routine. For the last three days, all she'd been saying was *Talk to your parents, this is so stupid, you'll be fine, how can they do this to you, I can't believe they won't let you play.*

His cell rang again. It was Griff. "Nick, come on, dude. Come to dinner. You're just gonna get depressed sitting at home. And since when do you care about homework?"

"I *would* like to pass tenth grade."

"Okay, but you're coming to the game."

"No, I'm not."

"Yeah, you are. I'll stop by after dinner and get you."

"What're you, my mother? I said I'm not going."

"All right, all right—you guys are coming to Jamie's, though. Right?"

"Guys? What guys? Oh—you mean me and the girl who just said 'fuck you' and hung up on me?"

"Oh, man. Listen, I'm getting you after the game and you're coming to Jamie's. You don't want to be home with your parents all night, do you?"

"Hey, they're probably going to the game, too!"

"No they're not. My mom already asked yours."

Nick didn't reply.

"Oh, I get it—Devin's going to the game. That's what you fought about."

"Yep."

"Listen, I gotta get moving. I haven't packed up yet. We'll talk more later."

"My mother *and* my therapist," Nick mumbled.

Griff laughed and clicked off.

*I haven't packed up yet.* . . . Nick shook his head, grinning. You had to dry out your equipment in between games, and Griff always left repacking his hockey bag till the last minute. He was the most disorganized guy on the team—forever leaving stuff behind, borrowing hockey tape.

Nick went to the closet and unzipped his hockey bag. His mother was always complaining about the smell. Funny, though—the smell didn't bother him at all. He rummaged around till he found a roll of tape.

He loved the ritual of stick taping, pulling the old tape from the blade, then starting over. Toe to heel, round and round, tight, smooth, fast . . . Never any bumps or lumps when he taped a stick. *Do mine, Tag?* Jamie would ask. Maybe Nick could make a career of it. Nick Taglio, professional stick taper. He roams the rinks, appearing wordlessly at locker room doors. Superhero to fumble-fingered skaters. The taped crusader.

He picked up his Synergy and sat on the bed. Carefully, slowly, he started the job.

When he got to Jamie's, Devin was already there. They both pretended to be far too occupied to notice the other. She couldn't break away from a conversation about ski resorts, even though she didn't ski. He just had to hear all the details of the game, even though he hadn't played.

Finally Nick went to her, and it had nothing to do with sex. He realized that even as he approached her: it wasn't sex, but something else he needed now.

"Hey," he said, standing at her side.

She gave him a sidelong look—seductive and surly at the same time.

"Feel like taking a walk?"

She shrugged. "If you want."

"Better get your jacket."

"I'm fine."

Outside, neither one spoke for a while. Nick thought she should start, since he'd already swallowed a gallon of pride. But her determined look showed that she was waiting for him.

"Sorry I jumped on you," he said finally, and she came back at him with a vengeance.

"Well Nick it just goes to show you're bugging out about this. I mean God you yelled at me just because I wanted to go to the game and you can't get your schoolwork done." Her words burst out like shots from an AK-47. "Everybody says you just sit there in all your classes and it's all because of this, because look you're just gonna be miserable if you can't play."

"Yeah, I know, but . . . it's my head, too, Dev. It's still pretty screwed up."

"Tsss. Oh my *God*, Nick. That was two *weeks* ago. How long are you gonna, like, milk this one concussion?"

This must be what it felt like to be hit with a stun gun: completely immobilized. His instinct was to lash out. *Oh, that's what I'm doing? Milking the concussion? So glad you cleared that up for me.* But he didn't have the energy or the brainpower to fight, let alone win.

She must have realized she'd gone too far, because she stopped, put her arms around his neck and pulled him to her. "Oh, baby. Tsss. You have to get yourself together. Come *on*. You're a fighter." She kissed him. "You have to fight this, Nicky. Promise me you'll talk to your parents."

"Okay." He sifted her hair through his fingers. "Nice haircut."

"Thanks. Brrr. It's cold."

"Told you to get your jacket." He pulled her inside his.

"Can you get Griff's keys?"

"Probably."

"You want to?"

He grinned his answer.

"Oh, yeah, what a question," she laughed, throwing her head back to the sky.

Later Nick listened to hockey talk until he could bear it no longer and wandered away. And when he found Devin paired up with Ramsey in a game of beer pong, he showed no emotion and didn't say a word.

**18**

Divide and conquer: that was the key to dealing with parents, Nick always told Brian. So when he got home from Confirmation class and his father's car was gone, he seized the time and found his mother, alone in the dining room with a cup of coffee and a box of Dunkin' Donuts.

"Hi," he said casually, taking off his jacket.

She looked at the clock. "You're home early."

"Devin had to go to Springfield. Family thing."

"Oh."

"Where's Dad?"

"He went grocery shopping, God bless him, and he took Gabriel."

*And now here's Nick, all fired up to crash your party.* . . . But when would he have another chance like this? He went to the kitchen, poured himself a glass of orange juice, returned and sat across from her. She was reading *Parade*.

"You know they don't even bake them in the stores?"

"What?" She looked up.

"The donuts. I saw them being delivered once. They just take them out of the back of a truck."

"Oh," she said distractedly.

"Didn't you think they baked them in the store?"

"*I* don't know, Nicholas." She looked back at the magazine.

He tried again: "You know any saints?"

"Not intimately."

"We're supposed to write a paper for Confirmation class. Choose any saint."

"Go on the Internet," she suggested, pushing *Parade* away, sitting back in her chair. Finally, he had her attention. "What about St. Nicholas?"

"What'm I, six years old?" he replied, and she laughed. "Then they gave us a form. 'What does your Catholic faith mean to you?' and all this soul-searching crap."

She shook her head in sympathy. "When we were kids, it was a few practice sessions in the church basement, memorize the answers to a list of questions and then they lined us up and confirmed us. Paper on a saint. What's the point?"

*You tell me,* Nick wanted to say. *You're the one who makes me go. While, incidentally, not bothering to go to Mass yourself* . . . But they were actually getting somewhere. Talking. In normal voices. *Don't blow it,* he told himself.

"They beat Brock Hall," he said, taking a second donut.

She gave a frown of surprise. "Really? What was the score?"

"Five–four."

"Wow."

"Yeah." He looked down at the table. "Apparently Mac gave this big pep talk before the game, 'cause he heard somebody say, 'We'll never win without Nick.' So he gave them this lecture: 'You *can* win without him and you will.' "

"Oh, honey . . ."

Nick shrugged. "Well, they did. And they will. If they can beat Brock, they'll probably make it to the playoffs."

She said nothing.

"I think I'll be better by then," he said quietly.

"Nick . . ."

"Mom, come on. I *can't* quit. Come *on*." He lifted his head, letting a couple of tears spill out, wiping them quickly away. . . . He was getting pretty good at this.

"Nicky, listen." She cast a quick glance at the door. "If it was only me, honey . . . I know how important this is to you. I do. And so does your dad, but . . ."

"But what? What were you gonna say, 'if it was only me' what?" His heart was pounding. Breakthrough. It was coming.

"Well, you know how the Italians are. How hysterical they get. It's not that I'm *not* worried, Nick, don't think that. But . . ."

"But what? What?" he said urgently. "Are you saying . . . you're saying if it was up to you, you'd let me play?"

"No. *No,* Nick, that's *not* what I'm saying."

"Then what? What!"

"Nick. Calm down. What I'm saying is . . . on my own, I might have been inclined. *Might* have. But the fact of the matter is, Dad and I have to work together. And with your doctor. And—"

"And they overruled you. Why? Why'd you let them do that, because you're a woman? Because Blakeman's a big Yale doctor and Dad went to college and you didn't? Is that why you just let them make the decision even though you didn't agree?"

"Nicholas, don't put words in my mouth." She pointed at him, leaning forward. "Nobody 'overruled' me. *I* was the one who wanted the second opinion. The doctors say, 'If it was my kid, I'd never . . .' And then what are you supposed to say, Nick? 'It's not your kid, so screw you'? If anything ever happened to you and I was the one who said 'Let him play,' how would I feel the rest of my life?"

"Oh—how *you'd* feel! As long as you have a clear conscience, who cares how Nick feels. Right?"

"Nick, don't badger me like some TV lawyer."

The back door rattled. Nick leaped up, but it was only Brian returning from church.

"Nicholas, don't you dare start in on your father the second he walks in," his mother warned.

"What's going on?" Brian asked, his face clouded with concern.

"She'd let me play. If it was up to her," Nick said. "It's because of *him*."

"Goddammit, Nick! That is *not* what I said! I—"

"I know what you said," Nick interrupted. "I *know* what you said." He shoved his feet into his sneakers.

Brian just stood there, his mouth hanging open.

"And you." Nick poked him in the chest. "Quit staring at me or I'll take you down."

"Hey!" Their mother flew through the room, grabbing Nick's arm. "Don't you dare!"

"It's okay, Mom, it's okay," Brian said quietly, and Nick went outside.

He set up his net in front of the garage door and got his practice stick and bucket full of pucks. Halfway up the driveway, he lined ten pucks across and started taking furious slapshots: *Thuck*. Score. *Thuck*. Off the post. *Thuck*. Score. *Thuck*. Score. *Thuck*. Off the garage door. *Thuck*. Score.

The Cavalier pulled up behind him and patiently idled. *Thuck*. Score. *Thuck*. Wide. *Thuck*. Score. *Thuck*. Score. Nick stepped aside to let his father pass, then lined up more shots as he parked.

"Hey, guys! How 'bout a little help!" he called in his Mike Brady voice, and Brian bounded down the porch stairs.

*Gallant always carries in the groceries. Goofus shouts rudely:* "I have a brain injury!"

*Thuck.* Into the snowbank. *Thuck.* Wide. *Thuck.* Garage door.

Nick tossed the stick and jogged to the house. But they didn't need him to stir it up; they were already brawling.

"—the second I turn my back, then I get to be the bad guy?"

"Twenty minutes to myself!" she shrieked. "Is that really too much to ask? He comes waltzing in, talking so sweet, worming all this stuff out of me like he's—"

"Like he's what, Kath? Like he's what? You're the mother, Kathy! What're you trying to do, be his buddy? 'Oh, it's not me, it's your father! *He's* the mean one.' "

She opened her mouth to reply, saw Nick and shut it again. "Come on," she said to the wop. She stormed through the kitchen, sweeping her keys off the counter, and he followed.

"Get the groceries!" he yelled over his shoulder.

"Watch the baby!" she said at the same time.

Then they were peeling out of the driveway in the minivan, leaving Nick and Brian staring from the back door in silence.

"Who *was* that masked man?" Nick deadpanned, and Brian started laughing.

"Watch Gabe," he told Nick. "I'll get the groceries."

Gabriel was standing in front of the TV, still bundled up.

"C'mere, you little jerk-in-the-box." Nick swept him

onto his lap, tugging off Gabriel's hat and mittens, then taking off his jacket.

*Bob the Builder* music was blaring.

"What's this show on, twenty-four/seven?" Nick lay on the couch, pulling the baby snug up against him.

"Bob the Builder," Gabe replied solemnly.

*Bob the Builder—can we fix it?*
*Bob the Builder—yes we can!*

"How good is this guy, Gabey? Can he fix Nicky's head?"

Gabriel crowed: "Yes he can!"

When Nick's parents returned, they were the soul of solidarity. *You misunderstood, Nick,* she said. *I didn't mean blah blah blah, I meant yap yap yap. Dad and I are a hundred percent together on this.*

*The PCS of the MTBI of the RHI of the ZXCVB,* the wop added. *Nick, we just can't keep having this discussion. You've got to move on.*

*You've got to let it go.*

That night, Devin called when she got back from Massachusetts. "Did you talk to them?" were her first words.

"Can I come over?" he answered.

"Sure."

"Okay, hold on." Nick headed for the kitchen. This was always a little power struggle, walking the fine line between telling them and asking permission. *And oh, by the way—I need a ride.* He hated that most of all.

Before this last concussion, his father had taken him out driving a few times. Nick had his learner's permit, but his parents said he couldn't get his license until he'd gone to driver's ed, because insurance was too expensive without it.

"Drive me over Devin's?" He put just a hint of question in the words. His parents stared at him. "Please," he forced himself to add.

"Will they bring you home?"

He sighed and left the room. "Dev."

"Yeah?"

"Can your parents take me home?" This was so humiliating—he swore they did it on purpose, just to keep him in his place.

"Well, my mother went to the movies. But hold on. I'll ask *him*."

Nick paced to the den; Brian was building a wooden train track with Gabriel.

"Oh my *God*," Devin said, returning. "He is *such* a loser."

"No?" Nick mumbled.

"Oh, he'll *do* it. But you'd *think* I was asking him to find Osama bin freakin' Laden. He might have to get out of his recliner, you know?"

"Yeah."

"As if I didn't waste *my* whole day with *his* family."

"Yeah. Okay, I'll be there in about half an hour."

"Nick, you never answered—did you talk to them?"

"I'll tell you when I get there."


"So, tough luck, huh, kid?" Devin's father said when Nick went to the living room to say hi.

"Yeah."

"But you can't screw around with the brain, Nicky."

"Oh, be quiet," Devin snapped. "Come on, Nick." He followed her into the kitchen; she gave him a can of Sprite. "So . . . ?"

"No go."

With a dramatic sigh, she leaned back against the counter.

He shrugged. "I tried."

"Well, tell me what you said," she demanded poutily.

Nick kept his temper and recounted the whole story.

"Well, *Nick*, you didn't *do* it right!"

The only possible reaction was to shake his head, laughing.

"No, really! What if you just said, 'I'm playing, end of story'?"

"Devin, what do you think this is? 'I'm buying the little pink crop top and that's final'? This is, like, a major health issue, Dev, and—"

"Phhh," she interrupted, waving her hand contemptuously.

"Well, that's how *they* see it. Besides, you think Mac or the school's gonna let me play without permission? You think I can just show up at practice and say, 'Screw my parents, here I am'?"

She looked away, rolling her eyes, tapping her foot.

*Okay. Getting absolutely nowhere in a colossal hurry. But don't fight with her; what if this is the night?* Her mother at the movies, her father asleep in front of *Cops* any minute now, her little brother . . . Damn. Where *was* Brat Boy?

Nick took her face in his hands and kissed her below the ear. Her sound of pleasure stirred the little man awake. "I'm trying to get through this, Dev."

"It's only you I'm thinking of." She wrapped her arms around his waist. "It was so sad last night, watching the game, thinking I might never see you out there again."

*Thanks*, Nick thought. *That's just so comforting.*

"I guess I just have to"—he shrugged—"try to forget about it. And concentrate on other stuff. Getting better, and . . . maybe I can get a job. Start saving up for a car."

"I like Cade's SUV. What does he have?"

Nick couldn't believe she'd bring Ramsey up at a time like this—more so, compare Ramsey's SUV to the one Nick owned only in his imagination. But maybe she was testing him to see if he'd blow up. Besides, if she was fantasizing about Ramsey and his Land Rover, wasn't it strange to be doing it with her tongue in Nick's ear?

"A Land Rover," Nick said, but didn't add what he was thinking: *Perfect for that pretentious dick.* "I want a Jeep."

"Yeah, I can see you in a Wrangler. Black."

"Maybe I'll get a job at McDonald's," he said. "And when you come up to my register, I'll say . . ." He pulled her against him. "Can I supersize that for you?"

"Nii-*iiick*!" She giggled. "Tsss. Come on."

They went down to the finished basement. She turned on MTV and they sat on the couch, pulling a comforter over them.

"Where's Brat Boy?" Nick asked.

"At Ryan's. He's getting dropped off in . . ." Nick followed her gaze to the DVD clock: 7:35. "Twenty-five minutes."

He slid his hand under her top. Her skin was amazingly soft.

"Nick, I'm not doing *any*thing with *him* up there."

"He's probably asleep already."

"I don't care. It just—" She shuddered. "It creeps me out."

*All right, when?* he wanted to ask. *Where?* How long was he going to go around with unnecessary condoms in his wallet? He'd even practiced putting them on—how pathetic was that? Still . . . *Don't push it*, he told himself. He remembered his promise to himself not to even bring up sex next time they were alone together. This was that time. Wasn't it? No . . . that would've been *last* night.

Oops.

Well, not too late to salvage victory. He put his arm around her shoulders. "Never mind. Let's just—" He reached for the *TV Guide*. "What's on?"

"Oh my *God*," she said, looking amazed. "What's up with *you*?"

The back door slammed; in seconds, Brat Boy's feet were pounding the stairs.

"Hello, Jerry," Dylan sneered at Nick.

"Hello, Newman," Nick replied. "I can't believe your parents let you watch *Seinfeld* reruns. What are you, six?"

"I'm nine," he snapped back. "And you know it."

"What're you doing back so soon?" Devin asked.

"Ryan's parents got mad, just because we made a teeny tiny little hole in the wall." He jumped between them, snuggling in. "Whatcha doin'? Huh? Huh?"

Devin swatted at him. "Go away, you little freak."

"Oh, did I interrupt something?" Dylan asked innocently, then turned to Nick: "Didja bobble her boobies?"

"Get *out* of here, you little a-hole!" Devin shrieked, and he darted up the stairs with a maniacal laugh.

In three to five minutes he was back with a bag of microwave popcorn. They ended up watching *The Simpsons* and *Malcolm in the Middle* with him, and then they put on *Scary Movie*, which Dylan had rented on DVD.

At the part when everybody in the movie theater gangs up on the obnoxious black girl and stabs her to death, Nick mumbled to Devin, "*This* is a tad disturbing."

"It's hys*ter*ical!" Dylan said. "Didn't you *see* what she was doing, Nick? She *so* deserved it!"

"Yeah, but . . . why'd they have to make it a *girl* who gets stabbed? A *black* girl, no less."

Devin rolled her eyes. "Nick, I think you're taking Diversity Workshop a little too seriously."

His cell rang. "Yeah?"

"Nick, it's after ten on a school night," his mother recited tiredly.

"It's after ten on a school night," Nick told Dylan. "Shouldn't you be in bed?"

"What?" his mom asked.

"I was talking to Brat Boy. Uh, we're kind of waiting for Devin's mother to show. Her father fell asleep."

"Where's her mother?"

"She went to the movies with her friends. It should be over by now, but Devin thinks they might've gone out for a beer."

"Honest to God," his mother muttered. "Out drinking with her friends on a Sunday night?"

Nick turned to Devin. "Honest to God. Out drinking with her friends on a Sunday night?"

There was a stunned silence all around, and then his mom said: "Nick, I cannot be*lieve* you just did that."

He couldn't believe it himself. He just sat there with the phone glued to his ear while Devin fumed, twirling her hair, and his mother raged, "What is *wrong* with you?"

But he couldn't come up with a snappy reply.

"I'm coming to get you. Right now. Be *at* the door, Nick, if you know what's good for you." She hung up.

Nick pocketed his phone.

"I thought your mom *liked* my mom," Devin said sulkily.

"Your mom doesn't like my mom?" Dylan asked Nick.

"Go to bed, Dylan!" Devin shouted—and to Nick's surprise, Brat Boy raced up the stairs. "I mean, God, so what if she's having a beer with her friends? Why's that so tragic?"

Nick said nothing. He felt like he was trying to breathe under a hot blanket, like when you're little and you make blanket tents in the summer.

"And I don't even know if she *is* having a beer. Would it be all right with *your* mom if *my* mom was having a mocha latte?"

"She's just teed off because she has to come out again," Nick finally mumbled. "She's tired. She has to work tomorrow."

"Well, fine, I'll wake up my father! He *said* he'd drive you home!"

"No," Nick said quickly, getting up. "She's on her way. Don't get him up now."

Devin followed him up the stairs. "*And*, you know, *your* mom's gonna *kill* you for saying that out loud."

He didn't answer.

"Why *did* you?" she asked.

What could he say—*I have absolutely no idea*? His mother *was* going to kill him, and he couldn't blame her. One good thing about his family was that his parents felt like they could say anything in front of him and Brian. His mom always bragged about that to other people: *Our boys never repeat what they hear at home.* So of course she felt like she could pop off about Mrs. Hayes being out with her friends. What would Nick tell Devin next? *My mom thinks yours wears trashy clothes and tries to act like a teenager?*

"Just . . . don't say anything to your mother." Nick took his jacket from the rack by the back door.

"No duh, Nick! I wouldn't want her getting all pissed off at *you. Or* your mom, even though she *does* think mine—"

"Devin, don't blow this all out of proportion," Nick said, putting his hands up to his aching forehead. "She didn't mean anything by it—it's just my big mouth."

Devin didn't answer.

He stared out the back door window. Clearly, his synapses weren't firing correctly, as Mr. Shunk said when somebody zoned out in biology. He was so tired. His eyes were burning from the brightness of the kitchen light.

Devin's mom pulled into the driveway, walked up the porch steps in her tight jeans and high-heeled boots. "Hi, Nick—are we taking you home?" she asked cheerfully.

"Hi, Mrs. Hayes. Nah, it's okay, my mom's coming."

"Oh. Well, it's good to see you! How're you feeling?"

"Um, I'm pretty good, thanks."

"Where *were* you?" Devin said. "We were supposed to take Nick home, and I didn't want to wake *him* up, and now Nick's mom had to come out and she's pissed off."

Mrs. Hayes looked confused and a little hurt. "Well . . . Dev, I—why didn't you wake Dad?"

"Why don't you ever bring your cell with you?" Devin shot back.

"I forgot it," her mom said in a small, apologetic voice. She gave Nick a what's-going-on look.

He turned his head quickly. His mom honked the horn as she swung the van into the driveway. "See you," Nick mumbled, and got out of there fast.

*Okay. Let her scream as much as she wants. Then apologize. Right up front, just say you're sorry. She'll be so shocked, she'll let you off.* He got into the car. "Hi."

"Hi, Nick." He waited, but even after she'd backed out of the driveway, all she said was, "Seat belt."

All right. What the hell was this? *Go ahead, dickhead. Apologize.* He looked at her face. Tense. Thoughtful . . . Scared? All at once, it came to him. She thought it was the concussion, not his big stupid mouth, blurting that out to Devin.

*Screw it, then.* If that's what she thought, he wasn't about to apologize. But . . . maybe she was right. His heart crawled up into his throat. Maybe it was true. Because he wasn't so stupid as to say something like that to Devin. Hotheaded, yeah—but this was a different situation. He hadn't been mad; still, the words had just . . . tumbled out. Like somebody was channeling through him. Where did the injury end and his brain begin? Was this him, now, forever? Not knowing who or what was in his head?

*Calm down,* he told himself. *It was just a fluke. There's nothing wrong with your brain. You're just an asshole.*

His mom's blue and white cloud flannel pajama pants were tucked into her snow boots. Ready for bed—maybe even *in* bed, reading or watching TV—when she'd called him.

At both ends of the day, he'd managed to shatter her peace into little shards. If he wasn't so mad at her, he might have felt bad.

# 20

The Web site about *The Old Man and the Sea* had everything Nick could possibly need: summaries, characters, major themes, even a section on symbolism. He clicked on it; teachers loved symbolism.

> Scholars have been debating the religious, mythical and Freudian symbolism in *The Old Man and the Sea* for many years. But Hemingway himself had this to say on the subject: "There isn't any symbolism. The sea is the sea. The old man is an old man. The boy is a boy and the fish is a fish. The sharks are all sharks, no better and no worse. All the symbolism that people say is shit."

Nick laughed. Maybe he'd like this guy's book after all.

"Nick, Brian, dinner!"

He logged off and went to the dining room.

Brian brandished a drumstick. "Popeye's!"

"Excellent." Nick rubbed Gabriel's hair. "Hey, little dude."

"I gah Jahwee Wanchuh," Gabe announced, sticking out his tongue to show Nick the shiny jewel of candy.

"Keep it to yourself, dog," Nick said with a grimace, turning his face. He reached for a paper plate.

"Hi, Mom!" his mother said brightly.

"Hey," he answered, taking a biscuit and a thigh.

"How was school?" she asked.

"Scholarly."

The back door closed; his father walked in, shedding his jacket. "Whoa! It's brisk! You know how your nostrils hurt when you breathe?"

"Yeah, thanks, we're eating here," Nick said, slathering butter on a biscuit.

Brian went into the kitchen.

"Coke!" Nick called.

"Mom? Dad?" Brian said.

"Water, please," she said.

"Ditto," the wop said, kissing Gabriel, taking a seat.

*Ditto.* Where did this guy *come* from?

Brian returned, distributing the drinks. "Mom, I need ten dollars for a field trip."

She sighed. "Another ten dollars. Honest to God, this is *public* school? Where are you going, anyway?"

"The Amistad Memorial, in a couple of weeks. For Black History Month."

"Save me," Nick mumbled.

"Excuse me?" his father asked. "*I* think that sounds interesting."

"Good for you. *I* think it's bullshit."

"Nick!" His mother shot a look at Gabriel, who was decimating a biscuit.

"And why is it BS?" his father asked.

"Well, first we have Black History Month, which segues right into Women's History Month. If you're a black *girl*, you get two months in a row. But where's my month? Huh?"

"I guess some people would say that every month is white boys' month," his mom said.

"Bull—" He caught himself. "Maybe that was true when *you* two were in school, back in, what, the Kennedy years? But should I take the blame the rest of my life?"

Instead of answering, his parents just looked uncomfortable.

Nick continued, "Let's see . . . Asians, gays, Indians, Latinos, I don't know, who else? Everybody deserves respect. Everybody but me and him and him." He pointed to each of his brothers. "But then we have Diversity Workshop putting us through exercises about the advantages of being a white male." He turned to Brian for help: "What are the advantages? *You* tell me!"

"Um . . . everybody looking at us like we're the scum of the earth?" Brian said with a mischievous grin.

Nick slapped the table. "Exactly!"

"Fine, Nick," his mom said wearily. "But *please* don't express those views in school. I'll be getting notes from the guidance office."

"I know. We wouldn't actually want to *discuss* race or gender," Nick said.

His father looked amused. "You're in rare form tonight."

"Yeah, I guess I'm all better," Nick answered. "Can I play now?"

"Let it go, Nick," his father said, trying to sound breezy.

This was what Nick hated. The wop found himself a

little catchphrase he liked, then repeated it till you wanted to strangle him. *Let it go.* As if it was that simple, a firefly out of a jar on a summer night. *Move on.* As if he had a destination.

"The brilliant sage," Nick said with contempt. "The answer man."

"Bri, please pass the biscuits," his father replied, and then they ate in silence.

Nick laid out his homework on the desk in neat little stacks: Spanish. Geometry. Biology.

Maybe he'd call Lucas. Lucas seemed to get all this stuff about zygotes and mitochondria. Nick started searching his desk for the school phone book.

In the bottom drawer, he came across a blue folder. Slowly, he took it out and placed it on the desk, then just stared at it. Finally he opened it and began to flip through the newspaper clippings, his eyes darting to the phrases he'd underlined:

> . . . *go-ahead goal came from freshman
> Nick Taglio* . . .
> . . . *Taglio scored two goals in the final
> minute, snapping the 2–2 tie* . . .
> . . . *sophomore Nick Taglio played a key
> role* . . .
> . . . *with 10 seconds left, Taglio wristed a
> shot that beat net minder Cox* . . .

A knock on the door. Nick shut the folder and stuffed it back into the drawer. "Yeah?" he asked casually. He was glad he was sitting at his desk, looking studious, as his parents filed in, wearing their worried faces, and closed the door.

They sat on the bed. Nick really wished they wouldn't sit on his bed.

"Nick . . . Vice Principal Weber just called," his father said, as if announcing a death in the family. "He said all your teachers are concerned about you. They realize it's only been a couple of weeks since the concussion, but they want to stay on top of things, especially . . . after last time."

"I'm fine," Nick said. "I just have to catch up."

"And they want to *help* you catch up," his mother said. "By using the resource room."

"Forget it." Nick got up, paced the few short steps to the opposite wall. "I'm not gonna go and sit in the resource room with all the retards."

"Nick!" his mother said sharply.

"It's only temporary, buddy," his father said. "They can help you get organized."

"I'm organized. See?" He stretched out his arms, presenting the neat desk: "Oooh. Ahhh. Organized."

"Nick—"

"No resource room. Keyword: no." He opened the door. "Bye-bye now."

They shuffled to their feet. "Nick, we *will* stay on top of this," his father said.

"You do that," Nick answered.

"I got you the banana pudding at Popeye's," his mother told him as she left.

Nick shut the door and lay on the bed, his head spinning. First they'd taken hockey away from him. Now they wanted him to go to the resource room with all the freaks and mutants who had to get pulled out of regular classrooms in order to learn anything. He would quit school first.

In fact, maybe that wasn't such a bad idea. He could

quit; he was sixteen. If he couldn't play hockey, why bother going to college? He could do construction, like his uncle and cousins. They'd teach him. It looked like a pretty good life, working outdoors, joking and swearing all day instead of being stuck in some office. Every night, practically, his cousins went out for beers with their buddies after work. And they always had hot women.

There could be worse ways to make a living. Like his father's, for instance. The stiff who came to the job site in a tie and a hard hat, taking shit from all the workers—and not making any more money for it, by his own admission.

Resource room. They actually thought he'd agree to the resource room. Live with these people sixteen years, and they knew nothing about him.

He sat at the desk again, taking out the fill-in-the-blanks biology sheet on topics the test would cover.

> A cell formed by the union of two gametes is a _____.
>
> _____ is an elongated cylindrical worm parasitic in animals or plants.
>
> A relatively stable state of equilibrium between interdependent elements _____

Nick looked away, rubbing his burning eyes. *Don't panic. The answers are in the book. Find the chapter and you'll find the answers.* But he couldn't even concentrate enough to find the chapter. Maybe he'd just call Lucas. Where was the school directory?

He opened the desk drawers. It wasn't till he saw the blue folder that he remembered he'd been through this all before.

Heart racing, he jumped up. He paced the room, and

stopped in front of the mirror. How could he look the same as ever, and feel so totally different? Where did his brain start and the injury stop?

He leaned closer to the mirror. "You in there, Taglio?" he asked, tapping on the glass. "Time to wake up."

Reaching between the mattress and box spring, he pulled out the smuggled bottle of Tylenol. He wished he had an ice pack, but didn't want his parents to see him going to the freezer to get one. He'd lie here just for a few minutes, then go check his e-mail. Banana pudding. That would give him a good sugar rush. Then he'd be able to get some work done.

He closed his eyes.

When he opened them again, it was 2:12 A.M. His head was pounding, and he was still clutching the unopened Tylenol, like a comatose drunk with a whiskey bottle.

# 21

If *a* equals *b* and *b* equals *c*, then *a* equals *c*.

Sounded simple enough. But how could *a* equal *b*? If *a* was an orange and *b* was an apple, how could an orange be an apple? The problem was that this one geometry theorem seemed to hinge on *a* equaling *b* and *b* equaling *c*. So if Nick couldn't even figure that out, how was he going to learn the rest of it?

Mrs. Chase tried to explain it to him after class, writing on the board as she spoke: "A = Nick. B = boy. C = smart. If a = b, Nick is a boy. If b = c, boys are smart. Then a = c, Nick is smart."

But all Nick could think about was that her next class would be coming in any second. And they would find him here, with *Nick is smart* written on the board.

"Nick?" she asked.

Voices approached. He grabbed an eraser and made chalk dust from the words.

Did she get it? She just stared at him, then said, loudly

and slowly as if talking to a deaf person: "Can you stop in after school?"

"Oh-kay," he answered, pretending to use sign language. "I'll . . . be . . . there."

Now she laughed, tapping his arm.

He felt weirdly dazed as he stopped at his locker, then continued to the cafeteria. He really didn't feel like sitting with the team. On the other hand, Devin hadn't exactly been warm and welcoming these last few days. Nick figured she was still mad about Sunday night, though she wouldn't admit it. He'd tried to get Alyssa to find out what was wrong; Alyssa said Devin was being "mysterious."

He bought a greasy slice of pizza and a chocolate milk and sat down next to Griff.

"Brace yourself," Griff muttered. "Ramsey got into Dartmouth."

"Dartmouth. Shit. He won't be skating for Dartmouth, I know that much."

"He says he doesn't care. It's the education he wants. He'll be happy just to get some pickup ice time."

"Yeah, well, that's about all he's gonna get at Dartmouth," Nick said, and they both snickered.

But Dartmouth, that was pretty impressive. Ramsey's father taught at Yale, though. All these Ivies were like a little club. That was probably the only reason Ramsey had gotten into Dartmouth.

"Hey, Tag!" Jamie called down the table. "I got the perfect sport for you!"

"What's that?" Nick asked casually, ready to ram the plastic tray down Chamberlain's stupid throat.

"Golf!" Jamie said gleefully. "You know, like *Happy Gilmore* golf!"

"Oh, yeah," Steve joined in. "You could get one of those hockey stick clubs like Sandler had in the movie."

"Can't you see Tag beating the shit out of everybody on the golf tour?"

*And I'll start with you two jerk-offs*, Nick thought as he laughed along.

"Hey, Nick, you coming to the Campton game?" Ray asked.

"Yeah, dude, you better," Steve said. "We're gonna need all the support we can get against those assholes."

"Tag, remember the last game with them?" Jamie said. "When that big mo'fo' had you up against the boards and you said, 'I'll shove that stick up your fat ass'?"

Could Chamberlain really be this dumb? "Actually, I *don't* remember it too well," Nick said. "Because that was the big mo'fo' who sent me to the hospital later that very same evening."

"Oh yeah," Jamie said dopily, and everybody else suddenly had other important things to look at.

"So, as you can see, that was a very effective strategy," Nick added. "You ought to try it with him Saturday night."

"Huh-huh." Jamie laughed his goofy laugh. "Sorry, Tag. I forgot."

"Whatever," Nick said, then muttered to Griff, "Who's got the brain injury here?"

It had been only the second game of the season, in November. His parents had insisted on taking him to Children's, even though Nick was sure he hadn't even lost consciousness. At Children's, they'd rated the concussion like a movie: *I'd give it a grade-two, Roger.* Blakeman decreed, from his medical conference in the Bahamas, that they should keep him overnight for "observation." His symptoms seemed to clear within days, and a week later Blakeman gave him the green light to play. In the next game, Nick scored two goals, two assists. And spent eight minutes in the box—a personal best. Slashing, cross-checking, roughing, hooking . . . Nick wasn't about to show his teammates, his opponents or himself that he could be intimidated by a concussion.

Mac hadn't said a word to him about it, but after the game Deke caught him by the jersey and said, "That was unbelievable, Tag. You got an iron set."

His parents had been disapproving, his mother thin-lipped and grim. But funny—when he was scoring, he heard her screams above everybody else's.

"I almost called you last night." Nick sat down beside Lucas in biology, laying the blank homework sheet on his desk.

Lucas looked down at the paper. "Zygote," he dictated. Nick wrote.

"Why didn't you? Nematode."

"Hey, no hurtful labels. . . . Couldn't find your number."

"Homeostasis."

"Let's not get personal, dude."

Lucas elbowed him; Nick grinned. "Exoskeleton," Lucas continued. "Hurry uuu-uuup. Here he coo-oomes," Lucas singsonged. "Microorganisms. Phyla."

"Homework, people!" Mr. Shunk called out, striding into the room.

"Myosin, epidermis," Lucas whispered quickly.

"Mr. Taglio!" Shunk barked. "It's pointless for Mr. Moser to give you the answers! You still need to know the material for the test."

Nick laughed, passing his unfinished paper to the kid in front of him.

"Any time," Lucas said, sliding a slip of paper onto Nick's desk.

Nick looked down at the phone number. "Thanks," he muttered.

# 22

Once again, Devin asserted her God-given right to go to the hockey game. She'd been a fan for years, she reminded him. Didn't he remember how they'd started going out?

How could he forget? Devin had been on his radar screen for a while at the end of freshman year. She was in his math class, but it had never even occurred to Nick that she could be interested in him. She was blazing—and he still saw himself as the doofus with braces that he'd been in eighth grade. He was grateful just to be noticed, like when she congratulated him for making the all-star team.

Then, in September, Devin and Alyssa had shown up to watch the first session of the power-skating clinic for hockey players. It was Nick's first time back on the ice after the grade-three in August, and he was feeling strong and happy. He saw her there but didn't think much of it. Afterward, in the locker room, Deke threw his arm around Nick's neck and said, "That girl? The blonde? She wants you, Tag."

"You're whacked," was Nick's response.

Deke had laughed. "Ah, you children. You know *so* very little. Nicky, she locked on to you like a heat-seeking missile. Who is she?"

And it was Devin who asked Nick out first, not even taking the easy way with an IM. She walked right up to his locker and said, "Want to go to a movie or something?"

He'd gotten over his shyness fast. They matched each other in mouth and temper, fighting hard—and making up soft. They were together all the time, just like Griff and Maddy had been since last spring. *You boys are too young to be so serious with one girl,* Nick's mom had lectured them.

And now here was Devin whining over the phone, "You're being a baby. Come to the game and support your team."

"It's really hard for me to sit there and watch, you know? Do you think, maybe, *I* could get a little support from you?" Right away, he regretted the words, so needy and pathetic. He hated hearing those things in his voice.

"Oh, I'm not 'supporting' you, Nick?" He could practically hear her eyes roll. "Just because I don't want to sit around and moan with you because *you* can't skate because *you* won't stand up to your parents?"

"Ahhh!" he roared. "Devin—have you heard one fuckin' word I've said in the last three weeks?" Then he clicked off fast, before she got the chance.

She called right back; he cut the power. How was he supposed to concentrate on this massive pile of work now? Burning with fury, he went to the kitchen for a soda—but as he approached he heard Brian and Jason laughing it up and found them making huge subs, with packages of salami and capocollo and pastrami and lettuce all over the countertops.

"Hey, Nick," Jason said.

"Hey." Nick opened the refrigerator, took out the bottle of Coke . . . and then Brian's cell went off. *O Christmas tree, O Christmas tree . . .*

Just as Brian was about to answer, Nick snapped the phone from his hand and started to reprogram the ring.

"Nick!" Brian protested, reaching for the phone.

"It's January twenty-sixth, lame-ass," Nick said, scanning through the ring options. "I'm sick of listening to Christmas music." He settled on the inoffensive Ring Type Number Four and thrust the phone back into Brian's hand.

"It's not Christmas music." Brian was frowning, his face bright red. "It's the Maryland song."

The University of Maryland was Brian's favorite basketball team. Nick filled a glass with ice.

" 'The despot's heel is on thy shore,' " Brian mumbled. " 'O Maryland, my Maryland.' "

Nick couldn't admit his mistake, so he said, "Oh yeah? My heel's gonna be on your face if I have to hear it again." He poured the Coke and left the room.

"What's *his* problem?" he heard Jason say.

Nick didn't hear his brother's words, but the tone—sympathetic, apologetic—aggravated him no end. How could anybody be as perfect as Brian? Someday, the kid would snap. Shoot a 7-Eleven clerk because the Slurpee machine was broken.

In Nick's room, sunlight was glaring through the windows. He turned the wand to shut the blinds, then looked at two framed photos on the wall, presents from Devin. One was of her and Nick at a party. She had her arm around his neck and was about to kiss his cheek, her lips puckered. Nick was facing the camera, saying something, looking raucous. He'd been pretty lit up, he remembered that much. Devin said she'd cropped out one side of the picture, where he was waving a beer bottle. *Nick @ Nite,*

Devin had written in calligraphy on the matting. The other photo was a shot of Nick skating in on the goalie, about to score. *In the Nick of Time*, she'd captioned it.

He turned away, sick with sorrow—and sick of himself for being such a baby. If he wanted to feel sorry about something, why didn't he start thinking about the 9/11 victims? Or, better still, the survivors? Right after 9/11, there had been all this talk of how it would change every-body's lives, make us better people. But now, only four and a half months later, most people hardly thought about it or talked about it anymore. All that remained was CNN's constant film of cleanup at Ground Zero.

He finished his Coke and set the glass on the desk. He was so tired, he thought he'd lie down for a while. Tired and cold. Pull the quilt up over him, just for a while . . .

Skating fast, the puck on his stick, his head down, over the red line, over the blue line, and then, clear as a bell, Griff's voice, shouting, "*Niiiiiiick!*"

Nick opened his eyes wide. His heart was pounding, and he was drenched in sweat. Still half asleep, he took out his cell and called Griff.

"Hey!" Griff sounded a little too cheerful. "Zup?"

"Um . . . I was just, I was wondering about something. Did you . . . the night I got hurt, did you try to warn me?"

There was a brief silence, then Griff said, "Yeah."

"I should've known he was coming, shouldn't I?"

"Nick, I want to talk, really. But I gotta pack up."

Nick looked at the clock: 4:10. "Oh. Yeah."

"I wish you'd come, dude. We all do."

"Can't," Nick mumbled.

"I'll pick you up after the game."

"No," Nick said quickly. Then, "Thanks, dude, but I'm staying in."

Griff sighed. "You fighting with Devin again?"

"I *think* she's fighting with me. But I'm not entirely sure."

"Nick, listen. Come over tomorrow afternoon, okay?"

"All right."

"Oh, shit. I can't. I have this family thing of Maddy's."

"Not a problem," Nick said, trying to sound upbeat. "Good luck tonight, okay?"

"Thanks, I'll need it. *God*, I hate playin' those jerk-offs."

"Just don't let 'em get to you, dude. Don't *show* 'em, you know?"

"Yeah. I know."

"See you later."

"Talk to you," Griff replied.

Nick meant to stay away from those newspaper clippings, but later that night—trapped in his room, Brian out traveling in a pack, their hockey-starved parents glumly watching TV in the living room—he opened the drawer and slid the folder onto his desk, flipping through the articles until he came to the one from the *Courier-Journal*'s special section on high school hockey, printed early this season.

### PROFILE: NICK TAGLIO
## Shoreline Sophomore
## Making His Mark

Nick took a deep breath, propping both elbows on the desk to hold his head in his hands as he began to read:

> "Renegades!" Coach Thomas MacPherson's bellow sends his second line onto the ice. As soon as Shoreline Cougars centerman Nick Taglio reaches the action, the puck is on his tape. No, wait—there it goes again. . . .

Score!

Last year, Taglio was leading freshman scorer in the competitive Southeastern League, one of only two first-years to be tapped for the all-star game. And now the sixteen-year-old is considered a force to be reckoned with.

"Nick has a remarkable knack for anticipating the play—he moves into just the right place at just the right time. He's fast and he's fearless." MacPherson chuckles. "Well, maybe a little too fearless."

Perhaps as a result, Taglio spends a little too much time in the penalty box—and the emergency room. His first concussion came last season in a game against Brock Hall. "It was a mild one, what they call a grade-one," Taglio says. "I just got my bell rung, and I had to sit out for the rest of the game."

But at the end of his two-week hockey camp stay in August, Taglio was involved in a serious collision that led to an overnight hospital stay. And in only the second game of this season, the intense, dark-eyed tenth grader spent another night under observation after a third concussion during a game with the Campton Dragons.

"I guess I got into a couple of shoving matches with somebody I should've tried to avoid," Taglio admits sheepishly.

"Nick's like a tough little dog who thinks it's a pit bull," MacPherson said of his five-foot-eight, 160-pound center.

Nick laughed, remembering how his teammates greeted him with barks and growls when he entered the locker room the day the article was printed.

> In fact, if MacPherson could change one thing about his budding star's game, he knows exactly what it would be: "I tell Nick all the time. 'You can't score if you're sitting in the [penalty] box. You need to be a little more Gretzky, a little less Gordie," Mac says, the latter a reference to Mr. Howe, perhaps the NHL's most famously fearless fighter. "Nick has the talent, the accuracy, the speed and the smarts to be an artist on the ice."
> Instead, "I guess I play a little too much in your face," admits Taglio, who acknowledges that hard-charging, concussion-prone Eric Lindros is his professional idol. "But taking penalties, getting hit . . ." He shrugs and shoots the visitor a disarming grin. "That's hockey," he says, and skates away.

Nick looked at the kid in the picture, so confident, on top of the world.

"That's hockey," he muttered. "Asshole."

He shoved the folder back into the drawer. *Remarkable knack for anticipating the play*. Right. That's why the Canuck—what was his name?—had been on top of him before Nick even knew he was coming.

As for Mac . . . his song hadn't been so sweet after the reporter left. "Keep your head up!" he'd screamed. "Do I have to tattoo it on your forehead?" Then he told Nick to write five times for homework: *I am not Eric Lindros, I am a high school sophomore.* Nick didn't think Mac was serious, but when he turned up at the next practice without the assignment, Mac made him write it on the locker room whiteboard.

Eight-thirty. Well into the game by now. Was Griff holding up under the Dragons' onslaught? Was Ramsey "stepping up" again—that phony jerk-off, with his stupid soap opera name?

Was Devin in the stands, screaming for him, jumping up and down?

Nick turned on the fan to block the sound of the TV. Hanging from his bedpost was a Teenie Beanie Bopper doll, a hockey player in red and black. Devin had given it to him for Christmas. She'd sprayed it with her perfume; for a week the scent had filled the room. Nick pressed his nose to it, inhaling deeply. Still there, but nowhere near as strong. Christmas Day, the little smiling face peeked from the stocking she gave him. Alone with her in the den, a few sneaked minutes, unable to do much except kiss, but her hand . . .

He locked his door and turned off the light. In bed, he reached to the nightstand for his CD player, adjusting the headphones over his ears. Dave was singing "Rapunzel":

*Take me for a ride . . .*

Nick shut his eyes and put himself in the car with Devin.

# 23

On Sunday, he refused to go to Confirmation class; Devin never called. He gave up on schoolwork and spent the day eating E. L. Fudge cookies and watching TV Land.

His family stayed away.

It wasn't till Monday that he learned the Cougars had beaten the Dragons 2–0, Deke and Ramsey with one goal apiece. Griff had shut out Campton.

"Shit," Nick said. "At *this* rate you guys'll definitely make the play-offs."

Griff shrugged. "I doubt it. This can't last."

"That's the spirit, dude! So, why didn't you call and tell me?"

"I don't know," he mumbled. "I didn't want you to feel bad."

"Oh, I'd feel *bad* because you pitched a shutout?"

"Well, you didn't want to see it, so I didn't think you'd want to hear about it, either. Especially . . . you know, Ramsey."

"I could have lived without *that* information," Nick admitted, and they laughed.

Mr. P. kept Nick after school for a "chat."

"Your teachers say you're floundering, Nick," he said earnestly.

"That's funny," Nick replied. "My *parents* say I'm crabby."

Mr. P. barely smiled. "I see it in language arts, too. You don't participate at all."

Nick shrugged.

"Are you reading the book?"

"Uh-huh," he lied.

"The paper's due a week from today."

"I know."

Mr. P. nodded. "Okay, Nick. Listen—if I can help you out at all . . ."

"Thanks, Mr. P.," Nick said briskly. "I'm just a little behind. I'll catch up."

He left through the side door so that he wouldn't run into the team in the bus circle, leaving for practice. He walked home alone.

As he was about to put his key in the lock, his cell rang. Devin. His heart skipped. *Just act casual*, he told himself. *Nothing's wrong.* "Hello."

"Hi." It was his mother. "Are you on your way home?"

"Yep," he said, shutting the door behind him. No sense wasting words.

"Listen, honey, Nana just called. Aunt Sadie's in the hospital, and Nana's got to go." Nana's aunt Sadie was about a hundred years old—literally—and always getting rushed to the hospital. "So she'll drop Gabriel off to you, all right?"

"Yep."

"Can you handle him?"

"Yep."

"How's your head?"

"Fine."

She sighed. "Call me if you need me. Dad says he'll try to get home early."

When Nana dropped Gabriel off, she kissed Nick's face, felt his forehead and gave him a container of roasted peppers. In Nana's world, a fever was at the core of every problem, and roasted peppers were the sure cure.

Also in Nana's world, boys shouldn't have to do any kind of housework and were entirely clueless about child care.

"Nan, I can do that," Nick said as his grandmother unzipped Gabriel's jacket.

She folded the jacket and put it on the counter. "Now are you *sure* you'll be okay, Nicky?"

"I'm fine."

She took off Gabe's hat, folded it, put it on top of the jacket. "You have to *really* watch him, now. . . ."

"Nan, I've babysat him many times."

"I wanna Jahwee Wanchuh," Gabriel announced.

"In a second, Gabey," Nick said.

"You have to cut them into tiny pieces for him, Nicky," Nana warned.

"Yes, Nan, I know that."

"You just take the end of the knife and—"

"It's under control, dude," he interrupted.

She giggled. Nick held the door for her.

"Good luck," he said. "With Aunt Sadie."

"Tell me what you think of the peppers" were her parting words.

Nick laughed to himself. She always said it: *Tell me what you think of* . . . whatever. As if her cooking was ever bad, or different, or anything but perfect.

"I wanna Jahwee Wanchuh," Gabriel repeated. "A pawple one."

"Gabey, listen: you have a substance problem." Nick took the bag of Jolly Ranchers from the cabinet.

"What?" Gabe asked, puzzled.

Nick placed the wrapped candy on the countertop and deftly crushed it with the butt of the knife handle. "What I'm trying to say is, you need an intervention about this Jahwee Wanchuh thing."

Whining, Gabe reached up, opening and closing his hand.

"Just this one last hit," Nick said solemnly, handing him a small piece. "Then, well . . . there's a twelve-step program for kids like you."

"I gah watch ShpongeBob." Gabriel ran to the living room, and within seconds Nick heard the Nickelodeon commercial music.

He opened the peppers and inhaled the good, garlicky smell. Since hooking up with Devin, he'd always been so careful about garlic. But today—not to worry. He sliced a slab of Italian bread, slathered on the peppers, and ate hunched over the kitchen sink, oil dripping down his fingers.

Just then . . . tap tap tap on the back door window.

Devin was standing there, peering in through a gap in the curtains.

Terrific. Slobbering like a St. Bernard, and not even time to brush his teeth. He practically choked on the last large mouthful, quickly washed off his hand and mouth, then went to the door.

"Hey." He wanted to seem casual but pleasant. Welcoming but not eager. He failed miserably, hearing that he just sounded nervous.

"Hi," she said, nervous right back—and as she averted her eyes, he knew.

"Come on in. I'm watching Gabriel."

"Oh. You are?"

"Yeah." He headed toward the living room. Surely she wouldn't do it in front of Gabe. Stay with Gabe, and avoid the whole thing. Later, figure out what she wanted, promise to give it to her. Just keep her from saying the words now.

"Nick, we need to talk," she said, behind him.

He sat next to Gabriel.

"Hi, Debbin!" Gabe said.

"Hi, Gabey," she said sadly.

But enough of such pleasantries: "Move. I watchin' ShpongeBob."

"Oh. Sorry." She stepped out of his line of vision. "Nick . . ."

He shrugged. "Talk."

"Can we"—she glanced at Gabriel—"go into the den or something?"

"I'm supposed to be watching him." He heard that his voice sounded young and trembly, and her yeah-right look brought him to his feet.

She turned when they were in the den. "Nick, I think . . . I just think we should, like, take a break for a while."

He folded his arms, tipped his head back. "Why," he said more than asked.

"We're just, like, *fighting* all the time."

What possible response was there to that statement? *No we're not. Yes we are. No we're not. See what I mean?* Or: *Yes we are, but it's your fault.* Or . . .

It didn't matter, anyway. She was ditching him. Well, she was trying. But he wouldn't let her. Figure out what she wanted. Fix it.

"Dev . . ." He hung his head to show penitence. "I know I . . . I act jealous, but I really, I'm really trying to—"

"It's not that," she interrupted, her voice steady and low.

"And about, you know . . . If you don't want to, if you're not ready—"

"Nick. Nick." She held up her hands, palms facing him. "It's not that, either. Oh my *God*. You're making this so *hard*."

"Well, what should it be, Dev? Easy? I love you." He stood close to her, trying his hurt, pouty face. She just looked away.

Now he'd used up all his endearing mannerisms, but nothing had worked.

"I love you," he said again.

"Things have changed," she mumbled.

Then it hit him. Finally.

*Things have changed.*

It hit him like that big Campton defenseman.

All her whining—*You have to play, talk to your parents, why won't they let you play?*—wasn't for him. It was for her.

How could he have been so stupid? Her boyfriend wasn't a hockey player anymore. No more Monday-morning bragging rights when he'd had a good game, no more drama when he was injured. She'd snagged an all-star. But now she had nothing but Nick, getting headaches, being depressed, having problems.

And Devin wanted to go to the game.

His laugh was more like a cough, and his voice came out amazed and amused: "This is about hockey. Isn't it?"

"You're making it so hard." She tried to walk past him. "I have to go."

He grabbed her arm. "It didn't matter . . . me trying to act better about Ramsey. Not be jealous. Not make you cry." He shook his head. "You didn't care about that. You would've taken that shit, again and again, if only I was still skating."

"Let *go*, Nick!" She tried to twist away, sounding panicky.

He released her. "How'd I miss this?" he said as he followed her from the room. "You wanted a skater. That's all you wanted me for."

Right in the middle of the living room, she turned and walked back toward him fast. "Oh, what about you, Nick? What'd you want *me* for, huh? My brilliant mind? My great conversation? Huh? You hypocrite!" Tears were streaming down her face. He was so shocked, he couldn't respond. She shoved him, then delivered her touching and memorable farewell: "You fuckin' asshole!"

Then she was gone, slamming the kitchen door behind her.

"Debbin's angwy," Gabriel announced, frowning. "Why she say?"

"It's okay, Gabey." Nick sat on the couch, pulling his brother into his lap, as if this warm little body could shield him. He stared at the TV screen, numb with anger and pain. She was right. He could not deny it: she was right.

*Things have changed.*

They'd been the perfect couple—the blazing blonde and the up-and-coming hockey star. It was a sort of pact between them, and he could no longer live up to his end. If she'd gotten fat or, say, her face had been mutilated somehow, would he have stuck by her?

*What'd you want me for, huh? You hypocrite!*

"Owww!" Gabriel protested. "Nicky, you *squeeze*!"

"Oh. Sorry." Nick got up slowly and walked in a daze to his room. Reaching under the mattress, he pulled out the bottle of Tylenol.

He kept telling himself to turn off the TV and build Gabriel a train track. But when Brian came in from basketball, they were still on the couch, staring at Nickelodeon.

"What's *he* doing here?" Brian asked.

Nick barely looked up. "Aunt Sadie's in the hospital."

"Oh." Brian lingered in the doorway, then went upstairs. Nick heard him walking around. Then he came back downstairs, stood in the doorway again, went into the den and walked around in there.

Terrific. Gallant had something on his mind, and Goofus was about to hear it.

Did Brian already know about him and Devin? Maybe she'd broadcasted it to the whole school before telling Nick.

Brian came into the living room again and sat on the little couch. *Don't talk to me*, Nick thought, clenching his jaw. *Don't even imagine talking to me.*

But Brian took a deep breath and said, "Nick, I just wanted to say, you know, I'm sorry about all this."

So he *did* know.

"I mean, I don't know if Mom and Dad are right or wrong, but, like, I know it's really hard for you, not being able to skate."

So he *didn't* know.

"I mean, I was thinking . . . like, I grew up playing in the stands in rinks, drinking hot chocolate and running around the lobby. And all that time I was playing, you were skating. Working, and learning. And getting better. And now it's just . . . all gone."

Nick looked at Brian, saying *enough* with his eyes.

"I know, I know. . . . But I just want to say, the thing is, as far back as I can remember, I've been Nicky Tag's little brother. Little Tag. And I—"

"Well, step up, boy!" Nick burst out. "Come on out from behind my shadow! Oh, what's that? I don't have a shadow anymore? So much the better. Mr. Mediocre, competent at every sport he tries, excels at nothing. Step up and shine, dude! It's your big chance!"  ·

Brian just stared with the coldest look Nick had ever seen. Then he said steadily, "I was gonna say, it never mattered. I never cared, because I always liked being your brother." He got to his feet and headed out of the room. "Forget you. You fuckin' asshole." The back door slammed.

Two fuckin' assholes in one afternoon.

Even by Nick's standards, this was a record.

Dinner was quiet; Nick and Brian avoided each other's eyes.

"How was practice, Bri?" their father asked.

"All right," Brian said with an uncharacteristic surly edge.

Nick saw his parents give each other a perplexed look.

"Anything interesting happen at school?" their mother said.

"No," Nick and Brian both mumbled.

"What's goin' on, guys?" their father said in his buddy voice.

Neither one answered.

"Well, how about you, Gabey?" their mother asked. "Were you a good boy for Nicky this afternoon?"

"Fugginasso!" the baby cheerfully replied.

Both parents inhaled like it was their last gasp.

"Fugginasso!" Gabriel shrieked, banging his spoon on the high chair tray. "Fugginasso!"

"Gabriel!" their mother said. "Stop that! That's naughty!"

"Oh, terrific, Nick, just great," the wop said, throwing up his hands in disgust. "We leave you with him for one afternoon . . ."

Brian's guilty eyes darted to Nick, then away.

"How many times have I told you to watch your filthy mouth in front of this baby?" the mick piled on.

Brian just ducked his head and shoveled in pasta. Without a word, Nick got up, took his jacket off the kitchen hook and went outside.

He'd been in the driveway with his stick and the net and the pucks for half an hour when the back door closed and Brian's steps crunched across the snow. As soon as there was a break in the action, Brian said, "Thanks for taking the heat."

"No problem." Nick lined up another arc of pucks.

"And sorry about . . . what I called you."

"It's not exactly your kind of language, Bri."

"Well, I learned from the master."

"Don't learn from me." Nick's slap shot rang against the metal post. "Don't learn anything from me, dude."

He took a few more shots as Brian watched. They all went wide.

"Devin dumped me," Nick said.

"*Really?* Dude . . . *really?*"

Nick nodded.

"Why?"

Nick leaned on his stick, looking his brother in the eye. "She was in it for a skater." He shrugged. "It's that simple."

"Oh, *man.*" Brian shook his head, looking disgusted. "That sucks."

"So that's why I was in not such a great mood when you came in."

"Ahh, no big deal."

"Do me a favor?"

"Sure."

Nick nodded toward the house. "Tell them?"

"Okay."

Nick set up some more pucks, and Brian went inside.

Later, Nick was scooping ice cream when his mother wandered into the kitchen and said, "I'll just make this one comment and then I'll never bring it up again."

"Please," Nick warned wearily.

"I always thought it was peculiar how much she cared about the hockey."

"Well, I guess you're some kind of psychic genius," Nick said, returning the ice cream carton to the freezer.

Then his father joined the festivities. "Nick, I know this seems like the end of the world right now, but believe me, in a couple years, it'll be an insignificant blip on your life's radar."

Nick put his bowl into the microwave and punched in ten seconds.

"We haven't gone driving for a long time," his father said. "Want to?"

"Nope." The microwave beeped; he brought the ice cream to the den and checked his e-mail.

From GRIFFBURROZ:
If it's any consolation, Maddy's really steamed at D. She sez she duznt even want to sit w/her at games anymore.

Nick hit *Reply* and typed:
It's no consolation whatsoever. But tx 4
sharing.

From MISSLYSS777:
Nicky I hope we can still b. friends. I think
she's CRAZY but she's my best friend, what cn
I do? LV U!

Nick didn't bother to answer.

All week at school, he took care not to be where Devin was. At lunch his friends had nothing to say to him, or even in front of him. Nick had the skin-crawling feeling that everybody was talking behind his back, saying . . . what?

*Did you hear Devin ditched Tag? Well, can you blame her? The guy's, like,* Night of the Zombies. . . . *Tag got a 30 on his biology test, even with Lucas trying to cheat him through it. . . . I heard they want him to go to the resource room. . . . Yeah, and don't you hate talking about hockey in front of him anymore? . . .*

Even Griff was acting strange, all big brotherly and chin-up-ish. But when Griff invited him over Friday night, he decided to go. He had nothing else to do, and he was sick of staying home looking pathetic in front of his parents and Brian. When he said he was going to sleep at Griff's, his parents' relief was embarrassingly obvious.

Griff's mom was in the kitchen, dressed to go out, when Nick arrived.

"I'm unique among my gender, Nick," was the first thing she said to him.

"Why's that, Laur?"

"Because I am the only woman I know who has to wait for her husband every time they go out. Jack!" she called.

Griff walked into the room. "Hey."

"No drinking, smoking or other illegal forms of entertainment," Laura said.

"Who, *us*?" Griff asked.

"Because I *will* know."

Nick didn't dare look at Griff. Their joke was that his mother always *thought* she knew but never did. It was Nick's mother who always knew.

"Now, Nicholas," Laura continued, "I have a bone to pick with you."

"Pick away."

"Oh boy," Griff said, rolling his eyes.

"Listen, honey, I know you're sad about not skating anymore—"

Nick twisted his fists in his eyes.

"—but you've got to give your parents a break on this."

"Exactly why, pray tell?" Nick asked.

"Mom—" Griff began.

"Griffin, Nick's been coming to this house too long for me to mince words with him. Nick, you know, it's not as if this is easy for your mom and dad. They're pretty invested in this hockey thing, too. And I know it was an extremely difficult decision for them. But they had to put your health first."

"So I hear," Nick said. "And hear. And hear. And hear."

"Never mind, Nicholas," she said sternly. "I give your

parents a lot of credit. To be perfectly honest, if it were me, I don't know if I'd have been able to make the same decision. To give it up. For myself!"

Nick laid his head on her shoulder. "Mommy," he said in a baby voice.

As Griff and Laura started laughing, Jack walked in. "What's so funny?"

"You guys are adopting me," Nick said.

Laura sighed, rolling her eyes. "Really, though, Nick—cut your mom and dad some slack, will you?"

"How 'bout—no," Nick said abruptly.

"Ah, you kids!" She headed for the door. "You're so clueless. . . ."

"See you, Nicky." Jack shook his hand, then rubbed the top of Griff's head fast.

"No funny business," Laura called, outside. "Jack, tell them no funny business."

"No funny business," Jack said, winking at them.

Griffin shut the door. "What should we do first, shoot some heroin or call the Oriental whores?"

"Watch your language. That's *Asian* whores."

They settled for going to Subway; when they got back Griff took out a pipe and they smoked some pot on the back porch.

Griff getting stoned the night before a game was a subject best avoided between them. It had teed Nick off ever since they discovered illegal entertainment. So they smoked pretty much in silence, then ate their subs, then went to the family room.

Nick sat on the floor, pulling out all the old video games till he found Wayne Gretzky Hockey for N64. "I challenge you."

"Oh, I will *so* kick your ass," Griff said. He hooked up the game while Nick untangled the controllers.

They had spent countless hours in this room, playing Gretzky and Breakaway, Tomb Raider and Nuclear Strike. When they were younger, they'd come back to Griff's house every Saturday after skating, settling in for a long afternoon of junk food and farting contests.

"Remember," Nick said as he got whistled for boarding, "how we couldn't wait to get to pee-wees and play like the big kids?"

"Whatchoo mean 'we,' white man?" Griff said, diving for a save. "Makes no difference to goalies whether you get to check or not."

Nick didn't stop playing, didn't even look at Griff. But he asked sarcastically, "Oh, did I say 'check'? Must be my brain injury, because I didn't *think* I said 'check.' I thought I said *'play'* like the big kids."

"Yeah, okay, Nick," Griff mumbled. "Same thing, though, right? Checking's the major difference between squirts and pee-wees."

"Whatever," Nick said, and they played in silence. But everything about the game annoyed Nick—the noise, the cheesy graphics, the way the light jumped around the screen. Was it the concussion? Or the pot? "Forget this," he said after a while, tossing the controller and rubbing his eyes.

"You okay?"

"Yeah." He put his feet up on the coffee table.

"So. You seem like you're all right with this Devin thing," Griff said. "I thought you'd be out of it. Ready to kill her."

Nick smiled, shaking his head. "I keep thinking about that song Dave sings: 'Wish I could bend my love to hate her.' But I can't. And I decided I just really have more constructive things to try for right now, you know? Like remembering the math I learned two months ago. So—" He made the sign of the cross in front of his own face, priest style, his hand flat. "Go in peace, you know?"

"Good for you, dude," Griff said—and there it was again, that patronizing, so-mature tone. "You'll hook up with somebody fast enough. Girls are always falling all over you."

Anything Nick said now would have made him look pathetic, so he just kept quiet.

"You want to smoke some more?" Griff asked.

"In fact, I don't," Nick answered. "And by the way, why are *you*?"

"What are you, my mother?"

"I just think it's fucked up. Messing with your head the night before a game, especially now that you guys could actually do something." Nick shrugged. "Maybe you don't *want* to skate in March."

"My mother *and* my therapist," Griff said, quoting Nick with his fingers.

"Think about it, though, dude. A win against Brock, a shutout against Campton. Oooh, maybe little Griffin would rather sprawl on the ice and cry."

Griff shot him a look of total disbelief. "Fuck *you*, Nick."

Nick laughed under his breath, staring at the wall.

"Yeah, *you're* gonna psychoanalyze *me* now? Why don't you look at your own life and ask yourself—" Griff caught himself and got up fast. "You want a soda?"

"Ask myself what?" Nick said steadily.

"Forget it, dude." Griff shook his head. "Want a soda?"

"Ask myself what, Mule?" Nick said. "You scared to say it?"

"Okay, ask yourself this: if *you* love hockey so much, how come you kept playing your same bad-ass macho game? Even after you knew you'd probably have to quit if you got one more concussion? Huh?"

Nick could not believe his ears. He shook his head slowly, staring at Griffin. "You fuckin' goalies," he said. "You have no clue. You stand there in your little crease, all covered up, watching, while the rest of us do all the work."

Now Griff was really heated. "Oh yeah? That's what I do, Nick? I watch? Fuck you." He started to walk out of the room, then turned again. "And *you* do all the work? You mean, like, when you spend half the game sitting on your ass in the box, while we have to play shorthanded? Or when you're—" Again he cut himself off, literally biting his lip.

"When I'm what?"

"Forget it!"

"No, go ahead. When I'm what? Standing around holding your hand?"

"When you're charging all over the ice looking for your next goal!" Griff burst out. "Okay? Ever since we got to high school, you're like a different person on the ice. You call me up and ask me if you should've seen the guy coming. The answer's yeah, dude, yeah. The guy got whistled, but you'd have seen him if you weren't so focused on showing off and scoring goals. Nicky Tag, the all-star with the Lindros style, is gonna get a hat trick in the tournament. *That's* why you got hit. *That's* why you can't play. So don't turn it around and tell me what *I* do and don't do when you don't know the first fuckin' thing about yourself."

Nick just sat there for a few seconds, letting it all sink in and reading the guilt and regret off Griff's face. Then he hauled himself to his feet. "Score," he said, heading for the back door.

"Nick." Griff sighed, following him. "Shit. Come on, dude, don't go." He hit the heel of his hand against his forehead. "*Shit*. I was supposed to be cheering you up, and—"

As Nick put on his jacket, he turned to Griff with a grin. "Failed in your mission?" he asked. "So, whose idea was it, anyway? Who told you to invite the loser head case over and cheer him up? My parents? Yours?"

"It wasn't like that," Griff said. "Nick—"

Nick opened the door.

Griff picked up his car keys. "Let me drive you, anyway."

"No. You'll miss curfew." The night before a game, everybody was supposed to be home by ten o'clock, when Deke and Zach got on the phone and called each player. If you missed curfew, you didn't play.

"I don't care," Griff said.

"That's noble of you. But I need the fresh air. The truth—it kind of stinks, dude." He pulled the door shut behind him.

Not a bad exit line. But all it did was put him out in the cold.

He started through the backyard, taking the shortcut he knew so well. *Your same bad-ass macho game . . . Nicky Tag, the all-star with the Lindros style.* The phrases had rolled right off Griff's tongue. Like he'd thought them before. Or said them before.

*You'd have seen him if you weren't so focused on showing off and scoring goals.*

Was that the Cougar consensus or just Griff's opinion? Was this how his so-called friends talked about him when he wasn't around? If they talked about his sex life, why not his hockey game? He wondered: what were their theories on why Devin wouldn't have sex with him?

Forget them. Forget all of them. He'd quit school and work construction with his cousins and uncle. No—not quit. Flunk out with a report card of spring-blooming F's. Get summer work in construction. Not go back.

It was all crystal clear now, and he had his best friend to

thank. Nick had never realized how useful Griff could be when he was stoned. He started snapping up his jacket, then all at once it hit him: off the team forever, and he was still walking around at school in his letter jacket every day. How lame was that?

At home, he climbed the porch steps and entered the dark kitchen. His parents. Jolly. Now he'd have to answer their questions, deal with their frowning concern. Best to get it over with fast. They were probably watching a movie again. He'd walk past, go right to his room. But as he reached the living room doorway . . . no TV light, just movement on the couch.

At the same time he saw them, they popped up like Gabe's jack-in-the-box. Still dressed, but . . . "Nick!" she yelped, adjusting herself.

His father smoothed his hair back, chortling like a doofus: "Huh-huh. Huh-huh."

Nick was so thoroughly repulsed, he couldn't come up with a single wise remark. Why would anybody do it on the couch if they were allowed to be in bed? He started walking toward his room.

"Pot." His mother turned on the lamp. "I smell marijuana. Nicholas—"

He sidestepped them swiftly and locked his door behind him.

A befuddled silence, then thumping on the door. "Nick," his father said. "Open up, buddy. I want to talk to you."

Then his mother: "How come you're back? Did something happen at Griffin's?"

"I'm going to bed," he muttered, tossing his jacket on the floor.

After they shuffled up the stairs, he quietly opened the door and sneaked to the kitchen for an ice pack, then to the bathroom. The fog was falling now, and as he brushed his teeth he could barely hold his arm up. He fell into bed, recalling his preconcussion regime of push-ups and squats every night. Would he ever be able to do that again?

Sleep saved him from dwelling on the question—and all others.

**26**

Nick was watching Saturday morning cartoons with Gabe when Brian leaned into the den, holding the sides of the door frame. "Hey, Nick, want to shoot some hoops?"

"Mmm . . . nah," he answered, barely looking up.

"Come on. I really need to work on defense."

"Too cold out there. You know it's Groundhog Day? The furry dude saw his shadow. Six more weeks of winter, dog."

"Right," Brian said crisply, pushing off the door. Then Nick heard his steps on the stairs.

Nick lifted his shirt and looked at his stomach. A month ago, he'd had a six-pack. Now . . . "What do you think, Gabey?"

Gabriel poked at Nick's gut. "Fluffy," he said. "Fluf-fy."

Playfully, Nick raised his arm as if to whack him. "Why, you little . . ."

Gabriel laughed. "Nicky, biwd me a twain twack!"

"After *Courage* is over," Nick said. "I love this one."

His father appeared in the doorway. "Hey, Nick, I've got

to go check on a job site in this new industrial park. You want to drive? It'll only take me a few minutes."

"No thanks. We're watching *Courage*."

His father left without answering.

When the show was over, Gabriel tried to pull Nick off the couch. "C'mon, Nicky. Twain twack! Twain twack!"

"In a little while," Nick said. "Look—it's SpongeBob!"

"ShpongeBob?" Gabe turned toward the screen, instantly mesmerized as the music began.

"Nick?" Hat trick! Now it was his mother at the doorway. "Would you mind keeping an eye on Gabe while I go grocery shopping?"

"Why can't Brian?"

"He's going over to Jason's to practice basketball."

"Yeah, whatever."

She hesitated, then said softly, "Nick, honey—is there anything I can do?"

"Get more of those little elf-guy cookies."

After she walked away, Nick tugged at his brother's sleeve. "Gabey?"

"Yah?"

"Did I just say 'Get mo e of those little elf-guy cookies'?"

"Yah."

"I must've been speaking in tongues."

Gabe didn't respond.

"You know what that means, Gabriel? Speaking in tongues?"

"Shhh," Gabe answered, stepping closer to the TV.

When Nick was skating, he and Brian always went to each other's games. But Nick hadn't been to one basketball game since his concussion, and today was the first day Brian hadn't even bothered to ask.

After the rest of them left, Nick walked around for a

while, seething. Over Devin. Over Griffin. Over everything. Stalking the house like a caged tiger, savagely biting the heads off little elf guys.

He noticed the letter jacket still on his bedroom floor from last night, and heard his father's pompous voice: *Let it go, Nick.*

Suddenly, he had a mission.

In the basement, he found an empty Gateway box and dragged it behind him up the narrow basement stairs and into his room. In went the letter jacket, first thing. In went the embroidered Gretzky quote from his aunt. Nick picked up hockey-player Jesus and noticed for the first time that Our Savior's right hand was low on His stick. What kind of a wrist shot did J.C. have? Nick tossed Him into the box. "Sorry, J-guy."

Here was the puck he'd caught last year at a Rangers-Flyers game at the Garden, with his dad and Brian. They'd had a great day, eating at ESPN Zone, shopping at Gerry Cosby's. On the train home, Brian had fallen asleep and Nick had had just about the best conversation ever with his father, talking about everything from school to hockey to music to Gabriel. He remembered his dad saying how proud it made a parent to watch his kids grow up and start to negotiate the world.

Nick tossed the puck into the box.

In went his first skates and the magazine covers of Gretzky, Gordie and Lindros. He took the Starting Lineup figures and the hockey magazines and the framed photos from Devin and shoved them in, too.

From his bottom desk drawer, he pulled out the sheaf of newspaper articles with his name so childishly highlighted. What a jerk he'd been, to think he was some hot prospect. In went programs from mites, squirts, pee-wees, bantams, high school.

There was a manila envelope in the bottom of the drawer; Nick pulled it out and opened it. At the top left corner of a loose-leaf sheet were the words:

*FOURTH GRADE—MRS. MILLER*
*SHORE HAVEN ELEMENTARY*

Over to the right was a gold sticker that read: *District Winner, Grade Four.*

### When I Skate
### By Nicholas Taglio

*When I skate, the whole world fades*
*As I go sailing on my blades.*
*Forwards, backwards, and then*
*I turn around and start again.*

*If I am feeling sad or mad*
*Or if at school I have been bad*
*As soon as I get on the ice*
*The whole world seems very nice.*

*I like the cold air on my face*
*And gliding at the fastest pace*
*I like to stop and watch the ice*
*Go spraying up like specks of rice.*

*No matter what the time or date*
*I'm always happy when I skate.*

*Not bad for a ten-year-old,* Nick thought, laughing to himself. Except for the specks of rice. But how strange—all about skating. Not a word about games, or scoring . . .

Long ago, before travel teams and checking and intim-idation, before cursing coaches and power-skating classes and suicide sprints that made you throw up. Before parents screaming "Kill, kill!" from the stands.

*When I skate, the whole world fades. . . .* And then I get taken down by a Canadian thug named Etienne.

*Etienne?* Nick lifted his mattress; the newspaper was still there. He scanned the story for the name . . . Etienne. Praise God, he'd remembered. He dropped the newspaper, and the poem, into the box.

It was nearly full now, but there was room for one more item. Nick took the Teenie Beanie from the bedpost. He brought the doll close to his face and inhaled deeply, closing his eyes . . . but then he saw her twisted, tear-streaked face, heard the words: *What'd you want me for, huh?*

He tossed the doll into the box and shut the flaps.

In the closet, he unzipped his hockey bag and found a roll of tape. He sealed the box, winding the tape round and round, till the roll was empty. Then he brought the box to the basement and stacked it with the Christmas decora-tions, way in the corner.

Four-forty-five on a Saturday afternoon. The weekend yawned rudely in his face.

Nick went into the den and logged on. For the first time ever, the AOL man didn't say, "You've got mail."

# THIRD

# 27

Monday morning, Nick heard the news he'd managed to avoid all weekend: the Cougars had beaten Nutmeg Charter, 4–3. He took a mean pleasure in knowing Griff hadn't had a great game, but still—it was a huge win, and it put the team one step closer to the play-offs.

Nick's teachers were buzzing at him about homework, papers, tests. His head started aching during biology. Then, in the hall, he came face to face with Devin.

"Hi, Nick!" she said.

He kept walking. How could she greet him that way— the way he'd heard her greet a hundred other kids when they'd walked the halls together? No guilt, no embarrassment. *Hi, Nick,* like he was just anybody.

In L.A., he slid into his seat and opened his notebook. Who'd gotten the four goals Saturday night? Had Ramsey scored? At practice, in the locker room—did they even mention Nick's name anymore? Did Steve and Jamie miss him on the line at all? If everybody agreed with

Griff, then maybe they were happier without him. But it couldn't be true, all Griff had said. If he played that way, he would have heard about it from Mac, loud and clear. Griffin was just jealous, he—

"Nick?" Mr. P. said.

He lifted his head. The room was dead silent, and all eyes were on him. His face was heating up. "Um . . . what was the question?" he mumbled.

Then, from somewhere behind Nick, somebody said in a retard voice: "Duh . . . my name is Nicky Tag."

The whole class burst out laughing.

"Who said that?" Mr. P. barked, striding toward the back of the room.

Nick felt himself blushing deeper. Options: sit here and let everybody see his humiliation, or get up and walk out—and let everybody see he cared.

"—how rude and thoughtless that is?" Mr. P. was saying.

"It wasn't me!" Pete Maguire answered. "I swear!"

"Then who was it?"

Nick shut his notebook, got up and slid his books under his arm, praying as he headed out, *Please, God, just this one thing: don't let me trip now.*

In the empty boys' room, he stuck his head under the cold-water faucet. Teachers were so stupid—always asking who did it. As if anybody would admit it. And talk about thoughtless. Nick knew Mr. P. liked him. So why would Mr. P. call on him when he could see Nick wasn't listening? Then embarrass him even more by making a big deal over who had ridiculed him?

And what was Nick supposed to do now? Hide in the bathroom the rest of the period? Then what? Finish out the day as if nothing had happened?

"Screw you guys, I'm goin' home," he said.

He made a quick stop at his locker, taking his backpack

and jacket, then walked out of the building through a back door. By the time he got home, his hair was actually frozen. Even the house felt warm by comparison, though they turned the heat down to sixty-four on weekdays. Nick cranked it up to sixty-eight and turned off his cell. He took three extra-strength Tylenol and an extra-hot shower. Then he put on flannel pants and the old Rangers sweat-shirt and brought his pillow and down quilt and ice pack into the den, where he lay on the couch and turned on TV Land. *Leave It to Beaver* was on.

It made him feel snug and safe, being transported to that fifties world. He dozed off for a while, and when he woke his headache was gone. He nuked two packets of Easy Mac and ate on the couch.

Nobody called, nobody bothered him. There were no prying teachers, no staring kids. He'd ditched school but learned a lesson: home was a pretty sweet place to hide.

When his parents filed into his room that night, Nick took off his headphones.

"Nick, I got a call from school today," his mother began.

"Say no more," he answered.

"Mom set up a meeting," his father said. "Us and your teachers, Vice Principal Weber and your counselor."

"Tell them hi for me."

"You'll be there, too."

"That's where you're mistaken."

"Nick, the idea is to get you back on track, figure out—"

"I'm quitting."

Their jaws dropped.

"Whatta ya talkin' about?" his father yelled, and Nick nearly laughed. Whenever his father got really mad, he forgot his continuing effort to rise above his working-class background and immediately started talking wop.

"I'm talkin' about I'm not going back to school."

"Oh yeah you are, even if I have to carry you."

"You think you can?" Nick stood up. "C'mon, let's see."

"Nick!" his mother said.

"You listen to me, you little shit . . ."

"Mike! Both of you!"

His father sat down heavily on the bed. Again, on Nick's bed.

Then Nick saw his mother notice that all the hockey stuff was gone. As her eyes darted around the room, she looked sad, maybe even scared. "Oh, Nicky."

Nick shrugged. "He keeps telling me to let it go. So I let it go."

His father shook his head and said with supreme scorn, "You're just determined to punish me for this, aren't you, Nick? It's all *my* fault, right? And you're gonna make me pay even if it hurts you more than me."

Nick rolled his eyes to the ceiling.

"My fault, your mother's fault, Blakeman's fault, everybody's fault but yours. You know what I should have done?" He flung up his arms. "I should've said, 'Sure, go ahead and play.' Then when you couldn't even stand up on your skates, you—"

"Mike!"

"Try me," Nick said quickly. "Go ahead and try me."

Now the wop switched strategies. "Quit school," he muttered. "Where you planning on living? Because it won't be here, buddy."

Ah, the parental power play: the old not-under-my-roof. Nick didn't answer.

"And how do you propose to support yourself?"

"I'll go to work with Uncle Jimmy and them." As soon as the words were out—and his father laughed in his face—Nick felt like a jerk.

"Oh, you will? You think it's easy, what they do? Like flipping burgers?"

"I can learn."

"All right, Nick. So tell me. When you're working construction and paying for your own apartment, who's gonna buy your clothes? Huh? Who's gonna pay for your haircuts and your cell phone and your DSL and AOL?"

"That's all you *ever* talk about, how much stuff costs. But hey—at least I don't have to hear about skates and sticks and helmets anymore."

"Whatever, Nick. You know what seems peculiar to me? Every time you argue with your mother and I, you've got all the answers. It's only when you have to do schoolwork that your head—"

"Mike!" Nick's mother said. "For God's sake!"

"Fine!" His father jumped up. "*You* talk to him, if you think you can do better! But he's going back to school, and he's going tomorrow, or he can move the hell out!" He slammed the door as he left.

Nick kicked the desk chair. "He wants me to move out? I'll move out."

"He doesn't want you to move out," she said wearily. "Honey, we're trying to help you, but you have to help yourself a little, too. You won't consider rehab, you won't talk to anybody, you're alienating your friends—"

"Oh, Laura called you? Little Griffin has to run to his parents with everything?"

"Nick, Griffin's been your best friend since you were five years old."

"You know what? I'm not talking about this. He's gonna threaten me to go to school? Okay. I'll go to school. You guys' end of the deal: get off me. Because I don't want your sympathy or your help. Can you communicate that to your spouse?"

She walked to the door. "My spouse," she said loftily, "happens to love you very much, Nicholas."

"Well, he's got a screwed-up way of showing it."

"Look in the mirror, my son," she answered with her Blessed Mother smile. "Look in the mirror."

With that dramatic exit line, she quietly closed the door behind her.

# 28

Mr. P. said, "Nick, I want you to understand that I in no way intended to embarrass you yesterday."

"It's okay, Mr. P."

"No, it is *not* okay. I really feel terrible about it, and I want you to know that."

This was even worse than the incident. Nick squirmed and looked at his shoes. "Don't worry about it," he mumbled.

"Yeah, I know, you can take it, right? Tough guy."

"That's me." Nick pretended to put his thumb in his mouth.

Mr. P. laughed. "You see, *that's* the problem. That's exactly the sort of thing I expected you to do yesterday. I only called on you to get your attention. I thought you'd just give me shit right back. Like always."

Like always. Except . . . "I'm a little slow on the draw these days." Nick raised his eyes to Mr. P.'s, grinning. "Try me again today, though. Maybe I'll do better."

Mr. P. gave that weak, concerned smile Nick was so tired of seeing on people's faces. "You know you missed the deadline on my paper."

"Yeah, I know."

"Your parents told you we'll all be meeting next week?"

"I am *so* looking forward to that."

Mr. P. laughed again. "Go to class, Taglio."

Nick concentrated hard all morning. He concentrated on his teachers so that nobody could catch him out again. He concentrated on his classmates so that he wouldn't lose track of conversations in case he got called on. He concentrated on the work, telling himself, *You can do this, just put your mind to it.*

By lunchtime he was all thought out, and he walked to the caf in a kind of daze, mindlessly joining the line . . . and then it hit him.

He had nobody to sit with.

True, he could go and sit with the team, as if they were all still his friends. But nobody had called or e-mailed him in days. A week? Longer? Griff had been his last tie to them, and now that was broken, too. He was sure Griff had told them: *Dudes, you should've seen how Tag tripped out on me the other night.* If Nick went and sat with them as if nothing had happened . . . how sick would *that* look?

As the line snaked to the cashier, he ate a piece of pizza and drank a carton of chocolate milk. Then he paid and walked out of the caf.

He had heard of a room where certain peculiar people spent their lunch periods in quiet and solitude. Perhaps he should seek this mythical locale, known to him only in legend. Perhaps he'd find comfort and shelter there, in this place called . . . the library.

He entered trying to look like he knew what he was

doing, walking straight to the fifth row of books and then studying them intently, keeping his back to the librarian's desk. He didn't want anyone to ask if they could help him. He glanced left. People were sitting at computers, using the Internet. He looked right. There was a bank of desks with high sides, apparently so that you could study or read in private.

Faking concentration, he selected a couple of books and walked to an empty desk out of the librarian's sight. He put the books down and slid into the chair, sighing deeply. Then he laid his head on the books and slept till the bell rang.

# 29

Seven teachers, one counselor, one vice principal, a school psychologist, a wop, a mick and a Nick, all crowded around a table so small everyone could see him sweat.

Seven teachers, reciting lists of all the work he'd missed, failed and blown off, while the shrink sat there staring at him blankly.

*Get Amnesty International. There's a kid with a head injury being tortured in the guidance office of Shoreline High.*

Now Dyer was talking—Dyer, who had always despised Nick, but acted so sweet and understanding lately. Hypocrite. She liked boys fine as long as they kept quiet and didn't cause any controversy, just the way he'd been since this last concussion.

"—and a final project for Diversity Workshop, due on March eleventh."

"Nick, have you been able to get a start on the project?" Ms. Weinstein asked.

"Nope."

She wrote, then said: "Mr. Polinowski?"

"Well, we just finished reading *The Old Man and the Sea* in language arts," Mr. P. said. "Nick's a little late with the paper."

"Señora Silva?"

"*Español* is about participation and memorization," she said sadly, in her musical accent. "And I'm afraid Nick hasn't been doing much of either. He has fallen far behind in my class. I give a quiz every Friday. Nick has failed every one since . . . his injury."

Okay, now they'd all taken their shot, even the music and computer teachers.

Everybody sat in silence, Nick staring at the table.

"Nick, I want you to understand, this isn't about embarrassing you, or putting you on the spot, or punishing you," Weber said. "It's about finding out exactly what needs to be done and then figuring out how to get you to that place."

Mr. P. cleared his throat. "I know I speak for every teacher in this room when I say I'm willing to help Nick in any way."

Nods and noises of agreement from the rest of the teachers.

"All right," said Ms. Weinstein. "Teachers, thanks, all of you, for coming in early." She tapped her legal pad. "Your input will be extremely helpful."

Seven teachers shuffled to their feet.

"Thank you all," the wop said.

"Yes, thanks, really," the mick added.

Nick started to rise.

"Not yet, Nick," Weinstein said.

Seven teachers filed out of the room. Hi-ho, hi-ho.

"Nick, what did you think of all that?" asked Dr. Anderson, the psychologist.

He shrugged. "I don't know."

"Mr. and Mrs. Taglio, what's Nick's status with his neurologist? Is he due for a follow-up?"

"Next Wednesday," his mother said.

"I was thinking that perhaps Nick might benefit from peer tutoring," Weinstein offered.

"Peer tutoring?" the wop asked.

"It's a community service option offered to academically accelerated upperclassmen," Weinstein explained. "We'd pair Nick with a junior or senior. They'd get together after school and work on whatever Nick needed."

"Well . . . *that* sounds okay," his father said. "Doesn't it, Nick?"

"Well, *sure*, Dad!" Nick said, mocking his enthusiasm. "Why, I always wanted to be somebody's community service project!"

His father gave his deep, dramatic, you-just-can't-please-him sigh.

"I wonder," Dr. Anderson said, "if we should let Nick go back to class. I'd like the opportunity to talk with Mr. and Mrs. Taglio on our own."

Nick stood.

His mother said nothing, but . . . "See you at home, buddy," the wop said.

*Buddy.* Was that supposed to show everybody that they had a close and warm relationship? A few nights ago he'd been ready to kick Nick out of the house. Nick shook his head as he walked to the door.

In his classes, his teachers were extra nice to him. At lunchtime, he slept in the library.

For Sunday dinner in Nana and Pop's sweat lodge, Nick shed his sweater and pulled a folding chair up to the table. He'd have to work fast to get the best food. In addition to his own family, his aunt Michelle was down from Boston, and his uncle Jimmy's whole crew was there, too. Nick reached for one of his favorites, broccoli rabe.

"Hmm, at Thanksgiving, I believe you were avoiding garlic because of a certain young lady you were seeing after dinner," Aunt Michelle said. "What was her name?"

"Devin," Nick announced, forking the greens onto his plate. "She ditched me."

"Ditched you!" Aunt Michelle said. "Oh God! Look at that gorgeous face! Is she blind or just stupid?"

"Both, I guess," Nick said, deadpan.

"Nicky, you come to me, buddy," said his cousin Jimmy.

"Just put in your order," his cousin Tommy added. "Short, tall, blond, brunette."

"Ah, he needs you two to get him a girl?" Uncle Jimmy put in. He waved a hand. "Get the hell outta here!"

"Yeah, Nick can get by on his looks, all right," his father said. "And I guess he'll have to, after he quits school."

The table exploded.

"Quit school!"

"Who—you, Nicky?"

"You gotta be kiddin'!"

"Oh, honey, what's the matter?" This from his grandmother.

And above all the other voices, Pop's: "What the hellaya talkin' about, quit school? I'll break your *other* head for you!"

"Oh yeah," Nick's father continued, "he informed Kathy and me he's quitting school and coming to work with you guys." He nodded at his brother and nephews.

"Mike," Nick's mother growled.

"Are you outta your freakin' mind?" Jimmy asked. "Smart kid like you?"

Nick looked across at Brian, who was staring cold hard death at their father.

"You wanna work with us?" Tommy said. "Up on the girders, sweatin' our *cogliones* off in summer, freezin' 'em in winter? Whatta ya, crazy?"

"You see that guy?" Uncle Jimmy pointed at the wop. "*He's* the boss. My little brother, he comes in and tells *our* boss what to do. You want to be like *him*."

Nick pushed his chair back. "No, I don't," he said, standing. "I never want to be like him." He walked out of the room.

"Nick-yyyy." The wop drew out the name, in his can't-you-take-a-joke tone.

"Oh, Nicky," Nana called. "Eat, honey . . ."

"Well, you deserved *that* one, Mike," Aunt Michelle said cheerfully.

"Yeah, I guess I did."

Nick went to his grandparents' room and took the CD player from his jacket, which was piled on the bed with all the other coats. In the den, he switched to the Winter Olympics on ESPN, muting the sound, and played Dave loud in his ears. Bobsledders were rocketing down the curved track as Dave sang "Digging a Ditch."

The song was from the Lillywhite Sessions. Dave was usually up, optimistic, kick-ass. Nick had read on the Web that Dave was depressed when he taped the Lillywhite Sessions, and that when he'd heard how dark the songs sounded he decided not to release the album. But the tapes had leaked to the Internet and were downloaded by millions of fans. When Nick burned the sessions onto a CD last summer, he'd been disappointed. The music was so un-Dave-like. But in the last few weeks, he'd grown to appreciate it, especially "Digging a Ditch"—all about how troubles and disappointments can weigh you down and make you crazy.

Nick pushed the remote's power button, and the Olympics went dark. Just a few weeks ago, he'd been looking forward to watching the hockey. Now he didn't think he could take it. He shut his eyes and listened:

> *'Cause I'm digging a ditch where mad-*
> *ness gives . . .*

It was like Dave knew his life and was singing it right into the center of his brain. Because here Nick was, alone in the dark little den with no idea who he was anymore, or who he would become—just like the song said. All he could do was sit here in his grandfather's La-Z-Boy, digging his ditch.

# 31

That same night, after they got home, Nick and Brian were watching men's luge in the TV room when the phone rang. A few seconds later, his mother was at the door. "Nick—it's a girl."

For a cruel second his heart jumped. "Who?"

But she said, "I don't recognize the voice."

Still his blood rushed faster. Deke had said, *There's a hundred girls who'd kill for the chance . . .*

He took the phone into the little front hallway and tried to say a smooth hello.

"Hi, Nick?" the girl said, crisp and businesslike.

"Yeah?"

"This is Kara Jensen, from the Peer Tutoring Program. I just wanted to say hi, and ask when you might want to get started."

He almost laughed out loud—at himself. "Peer tutoring?" he said, sitting on the stairs. "I didn't think I agreed to that."

"Oh!" She sounded surprised but not flustered. "Hmmm. They gave me your name. I guess wires got crossed or whatever."

"Yeah," he said dumbly.

"So, are you sure? A lot of kids end up liking it."

"I don't know. Nah."

"Well, I'm not trying to push you or anything, because, I'll be totally honest, there's a waiting list. But do you want to get together once and give it a try?"

And she sounded so nice, Nick found himself saying, "Okay. Sure."

"Great. When's good?"

"I—I don't know," he stammered. "Is it, like, after school, or what?"

"Yeah, usually."

"I'm good pretty much anytime, then."

"Well, tomorrow I have yearbook committee. What about Tuesday? Oh, no, sorry—they rescheduled chorus. Wednesday, stage crew."

Nick rolled his eyes. Did he really need to hear her entire college application? "Sure you can fit me in?" he asked.

She laughed. "Gotta get those community service hours or you can't graduate," she told him. "How's Thursday look?"

"Fine."

"Great. My homeroom teacher lets me use her room. Two twelve. You want to write it down?"

"Nah, that's okay."

"Just remember it's the boiling point of water."

"Wait—let me write *that* down," he said, and she laughed.

"Listen, give me your e-mail and I'll send you a reminder. Just to be sure."

"It's Nicktag826 at AOL."

"Great. See you, Nick."

"Bye." He clicked off but didn't get up. Why had he agreed to this?

*Yearbook, graduate*—she was a senior. She seemed funny, friendly, not like some know-it-all who would look down on him because he used to be a skater and she was— what was Ms. Weinstein's term?—academically accelerated. Maybe it would turn out she wasn't as nice as she seemed. Maybe once she met him and found out how stupid and how far behind he was, she'd be all superior sighs.

But Nick didn't think so. There was just something in her voice.

In the office of the big chairs, Blakeman rolled his pen between the fingers and thumbs of both hands.

"The exam we just did shows definite improvement,
but it's been nearly six weeks since the injury, and I'd
hoped more of the symptoms would have resolved by
now." He'd been talking mostly to Nick's parents, but now
he turned to Nick. "I've conferred with your guidance
counselor and read all the reports from school. I've spoken
to your mom and dad several times. They didn't want to
force you into rehabilitation on top of the . . . adjustment
of having to quit hockey. But now"—he leaned forward in
his chair—"Nick, Mr. and Mrs. Taglio, I'm going to strongly
recommend neuropsychological testing."

"Psychological?" Nick repeated.

"Neuropsychological," Blakeman corrected. "It's a series
of tests that would be administered by a neuropsychologist."

"What kind of tests?" Nick's mom asked.

"It's a full-day battery that measures just about every

aspect of brain function: cognitive, speech, memory, motor control, et cetera."

Nick's father was jotting everything down.

"What's the point of it?" Nick said slowly. "Other than figuring out *precisely* how messed up I am?"

"Nick, you're not 'messed up,'" Blakeman corrected. "Your technical diagnosis is mild traumatic brain injury with postconcussion syndrome. But people—"

"You got that?" Nick asked the wop, who was scribbling away.

"—do recover, in time. The thing is, the longer PCS remains untreated, the harder it is for the patient to adjust and recover. And the neuropsych testing pinpoints your problem areas so that you, your school and your family can work out how best to help you cope."

*Cope?* Now he had to *cope*? Nick's heart was pounding. What would they do next, send him to a group home to live with "others with the same disability"? Would he be taking the city bus downtown to spend his days working at Goodwill? *My name is Nicky Tag. . . .*

"I'm coping fine," Nick said. "No shrinks. No tests."

Blakeman was writing. "Rosalita will give you the card for the practice we recommend."

"Helloooo?" Nick held his hands at the sides of his mouth. "Am I in the room?"

"Three weeks is a reasonable wait under the circumstances," Blakeman continued. "If it's any longer than that, call me, and I'll call them."

Nick folded his fingers into a phone, thumb to his ear, pinky to his mouth. "Can you hear me *now*?"

His father gave Blakeman a secret nod.

Nick jumped up. "What, is this inappropriate behavior?" he said to the wop. "You want inappropriate? Here's inappropriate: fuck you."

He walked fast to the door; just before he slammed it behind him, he heard his mother say, "And *that's* exactly what *I* mean."

*What* was exactly what she meant? Nick stood in the empty hall and pressed his forehead to the door. The low murmuring of men, and then his mother's voice, clear, almost shrill: "But he *gets* everything. And you see, you *see* how quick he is!"

More low talk, and then silence. His father's soothing tone: "Kath . . . Kath . . ."

And then . . . crying. His mother. *His* mother, the toughest little mick this side of the Atlantic. Sobbing.

Nick walked fast to the waiting room, knees wobbly, feeling like he might throw up. His mother, crying. What the hell did *this* mean?

But she'd said it, and she was right: there was nothing wrong with his mind. It wasn't as if he was sitting there all the time with his mouth hanging open. He could follow the conversation if he was interested in it. Hadn't he talked to the peer-tutoring girl the other night like a regular human being? And he and Brian had been watching the Olympics together every night, talking totally normally.

Or maybe not.

Maybe Nick had been speaking in tongues. Then afterward the little dick was running right to their parents, saying, *You won't believe what he said!* Maybe nothing was the way it seemed.

Nick's skin felt cold and damp, like just before you pass out. Wouldn't that be sweet: his parents coming out to find him sprawled on the floor, Rosalita and her cohorts holding smelling salts under his nose. . . . He leaned forward, arms on his knees, head down, taking deep breaths, letting them out.

He heard his father's voice at the desk, and then his

mother's. Rosalita's gentle responses, followed by uneasy laughter. Nick sat up slowly—and caught another father staring at him. The man looked quickly away, but his little girl continued to watch him until the man distracted her. Nick realized with a sinking feeling that now *he* was the one being seen as the worst-off kid in Blakeman's waiting room.

Nick stood up as his parents reached him. *Sorry*, he wanted to say to his mother, but then she would know he'd heard her cry. She'd be embarrassed. He would, too. So instead of apologizing, he just walked by her side down the corridor to the elevator. His father stayed slightly ahead of them, Mr. Man, head up, chin out.

Nick didn't look at his mother. He didn't want to see.

When Nick stepped cautiously into Room 212, Kara was sitting at a desk, already at work. She looked up and smiled. "Nick?"

"Yeah."

"Hi!" She stood, reaching out as she approached, like a banker or a car salesman. She shook hands like a guy. "Kara Jensen. I thought maybe you wouldn't show up."

"Well, I had to keep stopping people until somebody knew the boiling point of water," he said, and she laughed.

But the truth was, he had almost ditched the whole thing. It would have been easy. He could have said he'd forgotten. The day had been excruciating—Valentine's Day. Giggling and balloons and flowers and candy . . . and Devin, down the hall with Alyssa, each holding a single red rose. They'd probably bought them for themselves, or each other. Just to make people wonder.

"So, how are you?" Kara asked.

"Beat," he admitted.

"Personally, I could not get through the day without my Starbucks." She rolled her eyes, laughing at herself.

Nick smiled, but he knew it probably looked sick, fake.

"Let's go through your stuff," she said.

They sat side by side, pulling two desks together. He sneaked a few looks at her as she sorted through his work. She wasn't hot, not at all, but she was no beast, either. Her skin was good and her hair was nice—straight, light brown. It kept falling down over her face, and she'd tuck it back behind her ear.

"What's your best subject?" she asked.

"I don't have one."

"Oh, come on. What do you like best?"

He shrugged. "L.A., I guess."

"You have Mr. P. He's, like, my favorite teacher here."

"Yeah, he's a pretty good guy."

"You did *The Old Man and the Sea*? I *love* that book!"

Nick stared at her. "How do you get to be this way?"

"What way?" she asked, pretending to be defensive.

"So . . . perky about school."

Then she laughed a really nice laugh, a happy and total laugh. "Well, that's one way of putting it," she said kind of shyly, and looked down to consult a typed sheet of paper. "This is a list of what your teachers want from you first. Mr. P. just wants the paper. Ms. Dyer wants this project for Diversity Workshop. How do you like *that* class?"

"Did you ever think it was weird that they call it 'diversity,' when the whole point is to pound it into your head that everybody's just like everybody else?"

She looked amused. She bit a corner of her lower lip. "That's a good point. You ever ask that in class?"

"Nah."

"Well, you should."

Nick didn't answer.

"You have any ideas for the project?"

"Nope."

She looked at the assignment sheet. "Keep it simple. To me, the biggest mistake people make is thinking they have to come up with some complicated idea."

"That's one fault I don't have," Nick said, and she laughed again.

"Try to think of some personal experience sort of thing. Teachers love that crap." Already, it seemed weird to hear a word like *crap* from her. "Oh, here's an idea! You're Italian, right?"

"Half."

"You could do something about Italian stereotypes. You know, how *The Sopranos* labels Italians."

"But I like *The Sopranos*. Every Italian I know likes *The Sopranos*."

"Then do it on that. Why do Italians like the show, even though it stereotypes Italians? You could interview your relatives and friends."

He shrugged. "I don't know. Maybe. Too much work."

"Yeah. If you think too hard, your teachers might actually believe you're *smart*."

Nick stared at her. "Where'd *you* apply?"

"UConn. Villanova. BC. NYU. I'll probably end up at UConn. The price is right. And my boyfriend's there."

She had a boyfriend? In college? "Did he go here?" Nick asked.

"No, he went to Lourdes."

Our Lady of Lourdes was the Catholic boys' school in West Shore. The Cougars smashed them in hockey every time.

"He play a sport?" Nick asked.

"He ran cross-country. He says he might try out next

year." She grinned. "How come you didn't ask if *I* play a sport?"

"Do you?"

"No, but you should have asked," she teased.

"You gonna go all Women's History Month on me?" he asked, and she laughed.

"Okay, proofs. Mrs. Chase says you're having trouble with proofs. So let's start right at the beginning. The minute you can't follow, stop me. *Don't* be embarrassed."

"*Sieg heil*," Nick said. As he watched her flip through the pages, he wondered what her boyfriend was like.

"Sadie Hawkins dance," Nick muttered. "That is *so* lame."

"Why?" Brian asked, putting on his jacket.

"Girls need a night when they're allowed to ask guys to dance? It's so 1950."

Brian shrugged. "It's just a tradition."

"Nobody's gonna ask you to dance anyway," Nick said, giving him the once-over. "Maybe when you get your braces off. And do something about your hair."

Brian looked a little stunned—then walked out of the den. Nick couldn't even work up an ounce of guilt. Why was Brian in here talking about this ridiculous dance when he knew how miserable Nick was? Besides, if Brian was too stupid to remind Nick that he'd gone to the Sadie Hawkins dance last year . . .

Too stupid, or too nice? Either way, Brian deserved it. If only he'd learn when to stay away from Nick, he wouldn't have to take abuse.

Nick checked the *TV Guide*. What was on the Olympics? Hockey, figure skating, hockey, curling, hockey, luge.

Luge doubles final. Excellent viewing.

His parents were going out to dinner with Griff's parents. Nick had agreed to watch Gabriel, who would be asleep by the time they left, his mother said.

Nick had a plan: consume large quantities of vodka, then pass out in bed before his parents returned. They never drank vodka, so they'd never miss what he used.

"You sure you're okay with this?" his mom asked, standing before the mirror to put on her lipstick.

"Yep."

"He's in bed. I gave him a little bit of Benadryl, so he should sleep like a log."

"Benadryl? What's the matter with him?"

"Nothing. I just gave him a little bit, to help him sleep."

Nick sat up straight. "You drugged him?"

She sighed. "Nicholas. I did not *drug* him. I gave him a tiny bit of a harmless antihistamine. I used to give it to you all the time, because you were always—"

"You drugged *me*?" Nick interrupted. "*All* the time, you say?"

"Oh, please. Most parents give their kids a little Benadryl now and again when—"

"But you said *all* the time. Not now and again."

"Nick." She turned to face him. "Don't break my balls. Gabriel is fine. Just peek in on him now and again, and—"

"Now and again?" Nick asked. "Or all the time?"

He was so incredibly bored.

"Good night, Nick." She bent and quickly kissed his forehead. "We'll be back around eleven, eleven-thirty."

"I'll probably be asleep."

"Fine. Just check on Gabe right before you go to bed, okay?"

"Okay."

His father didn't even bother to say goodbye. Since Nick had dropped the F-bomb in Blakeman's office, not one word had passed between them. But the wop had made sure Nick knew about the appointment with the neuroshrink, tacking a big note to the kitchen bulletin board:

NICK
TESTING
9 A.M. MARCH 6

Dick. How did he intend to get Nick there? At gunpoint? And then the place had sent a list of symptoms, which he'd left on Nick's desk. At the top it said:

**Please check all that apply every day until the day of your neuropsychological testing.**

Nick had studied the list, his heart sinking: *Depression.* Check. *Excess sleep.* Check. *Feel "in fog."* Check. *Feel "slowed down."* Check. And on and on, down through the alphabet. *Sadness. Sensitivity to light. Sensitivity to noise. Sleep disturbance.* Check. Check. Check. Check.

But Nick hadn't made a single mark. He'd only stuffed the sheet into his drawer.

As soon as his parents left for dinner, Nick put the vodka in the freezer. He flipped around the channels for a while, then fetched the vodka and a glass, filled it a quarter full, and drank it down. He shuddered. But then the warmth spread through him, and in just a couple of minutes he felt fuzzy. Not the fog fuzz of concussion, but the comforting, familiar buzz fuzz. He started to relax for the first time in . . . a long time. He drank some more. His parents should go out more often.

"Wus*sat*?" came a shrill little voice, and Nick nearly jumped out of his skin.

Gabriel was standing at the door in his fuzzy red zip-up sleeper.

"Dude, what're you doing up? I thought you got good drugs?"

"Wussat?" Gabriel came closer, pressing his finger to the bottle's shiny label.

"Good drugs," Nick told him. "Hey, you want to watch a hockey game with Nicky? Like we used to?"

"Yeah," Gabe said, hopping onto the couch.

Nick turned to the U.S.-versus-Finland game. With his brother and a bottle beside him, he felt brave enough to watch. But he couldn't keep track of the action; the skaters swirled. "You wanna play hockey when you get bigger, Gabey?"

"Yeah."

"Nah. Nah, you don't." All of a sudden a song popped into his head, and he changed the words:

> *Mama, don't let your Gabeys grow up to*
> *    play hockey.*
> *Don't let 'em . . . get CAT scans and . . .*
> *    walk on a crutch,*
> *Let 'em play . . . soccer and baseball and*
> *    such.*

He closed his eyes and tossed his head, doing the Willie Nelson drawl: "Mamaaaaa . . ."

"I wan Mama," Gabriel said.

"Huh?"

"I wan Mama."

"Your parents went out for a frolic, my good child. You

are under the care of your eldest brother, who will transport you forthwith to the princely bedchamber."

Looking puzzled, Gabriel grabbed a chunk of Nick's face, as if thinking, *Are you really Nicky?*

"C'mon, geek-o-rama. I better get you to back to bed. And you have to stay in bed this time." But when he got to his feet, he nearly fell. "Whoa. Gabriel, I think . . ." He steadied himself. "You should walk, dude."

"I wanna Jahwee Wanchuh," Gabriel said.

"If I give you a Jolly Rancher, you promise you'll stay in bed?"

He nodded, then followed Nick to the kitchen, requesting "a wed one."

Nick took a red candy from the bag. He knew he should crush it, but . . . he was tired. And the kid was old enough now to eat a whole candy. "Hey, you want a big one, Gabey?"

"Yeah!"

Nick unwrapped it and delivered. "Knock yourself out, dude."

"*Fanks,* Nicky!" Gabe quickly popped it into his mouth.

"All right. Now, upstairs."

Gabriel scampered up with Nick behind him, heavy-footed and light-headed. He tucked Gabriel into his Bob the Builder sheets, covered him with the Bob the Builder quilt. His SpongeBob nightlight cast a golden glow.

"Cozy room, little dude," Nick said. "You know this used to be Nicky's room?"

"Yeah," the kid lied.

Nick didn't come up here much anymore. He sat on the bed and looked around. He could still remember his father waking him up on hockey mornings by lifting him down from the top bunk. Walls of Ranger blue, white trim, red blinds, Ranger curtains and sheets and quilt. Even a Rangers lamp. Now the room was light yellow.

Nick got to his feet. "Okay, little doodle. You're gonna stay in bed now, right?"

Gabriel nodded, sucking mightily on his Wanchuh.

"Night," Nick said, rubbing his hair. He was getting pretty tired himself. Just a little more vodka, and he'd call it a night. Maybe sleep right through, for once, instead of waking up every few hours.

Back in the den, he poured more vodka.


"Nick. Holy shit. *Nick*."

He was late for a bus. His alarm clock hadn't gone off, and he'd missed the travel team bus, and he—

—was being shaken, someone was shaking him by the shoulders. Brian?

"Wuzza mar?" Nick asked, squeezing his eyes shut again.

"What're you doing, Nick? What're you doing?" Brian asked, sounding panicked.

"Sleeping," Nick mumbled.

"No, you're not sleeping. You're bombed."

"I thaw you were goin' new a dance?"

"I went, dumbass. I'm back."

"Didja travel in a pack?"

"Mom and Dad'll be here any minute and—"

"Leggo a me."

"Shit," Brian said. Then he picked up the vodka bottle and glass and disappeared.

Nick closed his eyes.

"Nick. *Nick*." Brian was patting his face. "How much did you drink, anyway?"

"Not too much. Jussa lil much. Now an' again."

"I better call them."

"No! I'm fine. Just gotta getta bed. I was aposed to be in bed. But I gotta lidda sidetracked, dude. Becuzzat baby woke up. You know." Nick pointed at the ceiling.

"You mean that baby, our brother?"

"Thassa one. You know she gives him drugs? You know that?"

"Nick, you're making *no* sense. Come on, go to bed." Brian tried to pull him to his feet.

"But he woke up. So I hadda give him a Jolly Rancher to get him back to bed."

Brian released him; Nick fell back to the couch in a heap. "You gave him a Jolly Rancher in bed?"

"Yeah."

"But you broke it up, right?"

"Um . . ."

Brian ran for the stairs.

"Wuzza mar?" Nick called, trying to start after him. But he tripped over the coffee table and found himself on the floor.

Brian was back in no time, holding the red candy between his fingers. "You put him to bed with *this* in his mouth?"

"I forgot."

"You *forgot*? He could've choked to death, you asshole!"

"Hey! Thass *fuckin'* asshole to you."

"Get up!" Brian slid his arms under Nick's and hauled him up.

"Izzababy okay?"

"Yeah. It must've dropped out of his mouth when he fell asleep."

"Um . . . Bri?"

"What?"

"I gotta puke."

Brian dragged him to the bathroom, raising the toilet

seat just in time as Nick dropped to his knees. The whole time Nick was throwing up his guts, Brian kept saying, "Good, you dickhead. Good." He walked back and forth, first looking out the window, then coming back to flush the toilet, then going back to the window.

"Am I dead yet?" Nick finally asked. "Because I feel rigor mortis setting in."

"Shut up," Brian said. "Are you done? If they come in—"

"Who cares?"

"I care. Okay? *I* care."

Nick struggled to his feet and staggered toward his room, with Brian on his heels.

"Just stay in here," Brian said. "Get in bed and you'll be asleep in a minute, okay? They don't have to know anything."

"Jussa lidda sidetracked," Nick said, falling into bed.

"Shut up, Nick," Brian said, pulling the covers over him.

# 35

Skating fast, the puck on his stick, but the ice is not marked with colored lines or face-off circles, and he's confused, disoriented. The stick's lie is wrong for him, the angle feels awkward . . . the puck slithers away. He looks up to see how much time is left. The scoreboard flashes 12:00, 12:00, 12:00 . . .

The blurry numbers on Nick's nightstand clock came into focus.

Power failure. He sat up slowly, head throbbing, and stumbled toward the bathroom. It was still dark out. Ice storm? His mouth was totally dry. He flushed the toilet, then went to get a glass of water.

The battery-operated kitchen clock read ten after five. Nick looked out the window. No storm, but plenty of wind. He shook out three Tylenol and swallowed them down, even though he knew nothing but time would help this kind of headache. As he turned to go back to bed, he saw his father's car keys sitting on the counter.

And it just came to him for no reason, what he wanted to do. It didn't seem like a big deal; he knew how to drive. And he'd be back before they woke up. So he got dressed, put on his jacket, picked up the keys and quietly closed the kitchen door behind him.

The streets were nearly empty. He made sure to drive the speed limit and stop at every yellow light. His teeth chattered violently until the car warmed up.

In about ten minutes, he pulled into the empty rink lot, parked and waited.

Soon the early birds started to arrive, the go-getters, two dads to an SUV, emerging with steaming cardboard cups of coffee, a gang of boys tumbling out both back doors. Then up went the liftbacks and out came the hockey bags, the kids running ahead with their sticks as the fathers joined forces, Booster Club presidents of tomorrow, joking and laughing. Five-thirty A.M.? Who cared? This was when the mites got their ice time; that was the way it always had been. As you got older, your games got later. Prime ice time was for kids Nick's age. When you were old and skating with the middle-aged men, you came at one, two o'clock in the morning.

A woman parked at the rink entrance and unloaded her little boy and his gear. They dashed inside, then she hurried back out and drove off.

Some families came all together, Mom, Dad and kids, getting out of their cars with blankets and thermoses and bags of Dunkin' Donuts. These were the ones who had two, even three kids in youth hockey. They arrived early and stayed late, staking out their turf, camping in the stands with the other parents.

Nick's parents had breathed a sigh of relief when Brian announced after half a season in mites that he didn't like playing hockey. For starters, they said, they didn't know how they'd ever have been able to afford two.

A boy dashed across the parking lot to his friend, the two of them jumping on each other like puppies. Nick couldn't help smiling. All at once he remembered it so clearly—that joy, that energy, the anticipation of getting on the ice and skating with his friends.

With Griffin.

The dashboard clock said 5:32. Everybody was inside now. Nick started the car.

But just as he was about to shift into drive, a minivan jerked into a parking space. The father leaped out and ran around to open the slider. He leaned way into the van, and then he was straightening up with a sleeping mite in his arms.

The little boy was suited up, skates and all. His head bobbed as the guy, balancing kid and stick, shut the slider. Just before he headed for the rink, the dad turned his face and kissed the kid's hair.

Nick watched them go, pressing his face to the cold window. And then he started to cry.

It was one thing to squeeze out a few tears to get sex from Devin or sympathy from his mother. But to be sitting alone in a parked car, sobbing uncontrollably with his head on the steering wheel, just because of a few little kids in their hockey gear—that was pathetic.

And it proved beyond the shadow of a doubt: his brain was permanently, totally and irreversibly damaged.


"You are *so* busted, pal."

Nick tossed the keys on the counter. "Oh wow, pal. Your slang is *so* Y2K." *Get away from me*, he was thinking. *Just shut up and let me go back to bed*. What were they all doing up, anyway? It was barely six, and here were the three of them, pale and grim in the sick kitchen light. His father was dressed, even had his shoes on.

Nick started toward his room, but the wop held out an arm. Nick stopped short. If his father even touched him, Nick didn't know what he might do.

"Where the hell were you?"

"You're always asking if I want to drive." Nick shrugged. "I wanted to drive."

"What the fuck's your problem, Nick? First you drink half a bottle of vodka when you're supposed to be—"

Nick shot a look at Brian.

"Don't give him that accusing look!" the wop yelled. "We figured it out! *He* tried to protect you!"

"The CIA's looking for people," Nick said. "Go for it."

"You know what, Nick? I'm sick of your mouth. You were supposed to be taking care of your little brother, and—"

"Take care of him yourself!" Nick shot back. "Did I ask you to have him? Did I?"

His father grabbed him by the shirt.

"Mike!" his mother shrieked.

"Oh, you're gonna hit me? Go ahead, big guy." Nick shook free and slapped his own chest with both hands. "Hit me!"

The wop shoved a finger in Nick's face. "You're on thin ice, buddy."

"Thin ice? No! I'm on *no* ice, thanks to you! What're you gonna do, *Dad*, ground me? Yeah, *that*'ll hurt. You gonna take away my cell? Here!" He pulled the phone from his pocket and flung it—Brian made a catch like he only dreamed of on the baseball field. Nick said to his father, "What a sad day for the little man. There's not a fuckin' thing he can do to me." He started to walk past, intentionally bumping his father, who grabbed him by the arm. They glared at each other, their faces inches apart.

"Mike," his mother said, her voice shaking. "Nicky."

Then Brian broke in: "Leave him alone, Dad." He pushed their father away from Nick. "Don't you get it? Don't you get it?" Brian's face was all twisted and red—exactly, Nick realized, like when he was little and trying to be brave. But he couldn't be brave now. "You're so *stupid*!" he choked out, and leaned on the kitchen counter, crying with his head in his hands.

"Bri . . . ," the wop said.

Nick escaped to his room, locking the door.

He dropped onto the edge of the bed, feeling . . . It was so weird. He felt just the way he did after his very first concussion, last winter. The grade-one, when he'd sat on the bench in a daze.

*Don't you get it?* Now what did *that* mean—did even Brian believe he was toast?

Nick looked at his hands, resting on his knees. A lump welled up in his throat. The hands, back and forth. The knees, up and down. Shaking. Like Muhammad Ali? Or like a scared kid?

His eyes were throbbing; he felt like his skull was about to split open.

*Endangered the life of your baby brother?* Check.

*Stole your father's car, and without a license?* Check.

*Made your other brother cry?* Check.

*Terrified your mother?* Check.

*Almost decked your father?* Check.

*Destroying everything in your path, like a suicide bomber?* Check.

Nick got into bed and pulled the blankets up to his chin, then over his head. His ditch was dug. *This is the bottom,* he thought. *It has to be.*

He was already awake when Brian poked his head in.

"Ever think of knocking?" Nick asked.

Brian shut the door behind him. "I just wanted to say, you know, about the vodka? I didn't tell them."

"I know."

"And the thing with Gabe?"

Nick looked at him fast.

"I didn't tell them that either, but they know."

"How?"

"The kid whistled you, dude," Brian said, grinning. "This morning he says to Mom, 'I wanna Jahwee Wanchuh. A *big* one, wike Nicky gave me.'"

"Shit," Nick mumbled.

Brian walked to the window and started dicking around with the blind cords. "And also? Sorry about before. In the kitchen."

"Bri . . ." Nick shook his head, snickering. "*You're* sorry? For what?"

"You know. Being a gaywad."

"You're not a gaywad, Brian."

Brian kept playing with the blinds.

"Anyway, how was the dance?"

"Oh, it was . . ." He shrugged, but his face was coloring up.

"C'mon," Nick said. "Details. Let me live vicariously."

"Well . . . there's this girl? She's in my English class."

"Name?"

"Emma."

"And?"

"Well, her friend told Jason to find out if I liked her, because she liked me."

"Liked *you*?" Nick said.

"Yeah, can you believe it? So I said I did. So last night she asked me to dance. And then . . . well, I asked her out. And she said *yes!*"

"Dude!" Nick raised his fist; Brian tapped it with his own.

"Nick, I was so uncool," Brian admitted, laughing sheepishly. "I was like, 'How about tomorrow?' "

"Ouch."

"I know! Jason was like, 'Where'd *you* go to clown school?' " He shook his head. "But I made a decent recovery. 'Cause she said she couldn't, how about next Friday? But instead of jumping all over it, I was like, no, I have plans, how about Saturday?"

"Good, good. Where you gonna go? How you gonna get there?"

"I don't know. Me and Jason'll figure all that out."

*Jason?* Nick thought: *Why don't you ask me? What does Jason know about girls?* "So . . . what's she like?"

"She's really nice. I mean, she's not what you would call hot. But she's smart and funny and she plays an instrument. You know, she carries around one of those little—" He shaped the case with his hands. "Like a violin or something. And she's sort of quiet, but when she says something in class, it's always right on target, you know, the teacher's always like, 'Exactly.' And I don't know why she likes me. I mean"—he shrugged—"look at me. And it's not like I'm great at any sport or anything. I said to Jay, I guess she must just *like* me like me, because there's no *reason* to like me!"

Nick just stared at him.

"I mean, girls like *you* because you're good-looking and—" He cut himself off, his eyes darting away from Nick's. "Oh, God. I'm such a jerk."

Nick shrugged. "Payback."

"Nick, that was not payback. For anything. I mean—"

"It's okay, Brian."

"Because I'm sure Devin—"

"Brian."

"—and other girls would—"

"Cut your losses, dude."

Brian shut his mouth. "Yeah," he said, and left.

So this was how Brian saw him: just a good-looking jock. No wonder Brian didn't ask him for advice—he didn't want anything Nick was selling. Nick couldn't help him with smart, nice, instrument-playing Emma.

*She's not what you would call hot.* When Brian said it, Nick heard the "you" as in "anybody." Now he realized Brian meant "you" as in "Nick." Brian felt he had to apologize for, or explain away, the unhotness of this girl he liked. This Emma who was always right on target in class. Nick thought of peer-tutoring, yearbook-staffing, chorus-singing Kara. Girls who didn't care how many goals you scored.

*She must just* like *me like me, because there's no* reason *to like me.*

Nick got up and walked to the mirror, staring hard into his own eyes.

His father had gone out at some point, and he stayed out. His mother pretended nothing was wrong, just bustled around, cleaning the house, doing laundry, taking Gabriel out, chatting cheerfully on the phone.

Nick tried to do homework, but everything he thought Kara had taught him about geometry was lost again, and it scared him so much he decided to go for a walk.

It had gotten a lot colder in the past few days. He pulled up his hood, shoved his hands in his jacket pockets and walked fast, surprised to find that it actually felt good. After a while, the Cavalier sidled up to the curb. His father rolled down the window and held up a paper bag. "Dominic's. Hungry?"

"I could eat," Nick said.

"Come on."

If he got in, he'd be trapped into hearing the heartfelt, man-to-man lecture. But if he refused, it would just make things worse. He hesitated, then walked around to the passenger's side.

His father drove to Shoreline Point and parked, leaving the motor running for the heat. He reached into the bag and handed Nick a root beer and a sandwich. "No hots" was written in black marker on the white paper.

"Thanks," Nick said.

Dom made his sandwiches on panini rolls with prosciutto, capocollo and imported provolone. A little shredded lettuce, tomato, olive oil . . . and Nick liked his with only sweet peppers. One bite, and you felt better.

"Nicky, that just can't happen again," his father said after a while.

*You mean the drinking or the car stealing or the scene in the kitchen or—?* "I know," Nick said.

"We have to find a new way to be with each other."

"Yep."

"You're agreeing?" His father sounded skeptical.

"Yep." Then Nick arranged and rearranged some words in his head before forcing them out: "Sorry for what I said at Blakeman's."

"Okay." His dad nodded. "Thanks. . . . Nick, I feel like I don't know you too well these days, but if there's one thing I'm still sure of, it's that you love Gabriel very much. And if anything ever happened to him—especially on your watch—you'd be devastated."

Nick pictured his brother as he'd left him last night, lying on his back, sucking the candy. *Knock yourself out, dude.* . . . He flinched. "I know."

A few more minutes passed before his father said, "I like these panini rolls. Do you? Or do you like the way Dominic senior used to make them?"

"These are better."

"Junior says his dad's rolling in his grave: 'Whatsis paneeni crap?'"

Nick laughed. "But I don't know how you can eat it with all those hots. It just kills the taste."

"No, no, no! It *enhances* the taste."

They finished their sandwiches, and his father backed out of the parking space. Nick was thinking this might actually have a decent ending. But as he shifted into drive, his father just had to say, "Remember when we used to like each other?"

Nick shook his head and turned away, staring out the window.

Kara told him not to worry about forgetting the geometry. "Two steps forward, one step back," she said. She was right; he *was* able to pick it up again pretty fast working with her on Monday, so he felt hopeful.

Then on Tuesday, in the library at lunchtime, he got the idea for the diversity project. It just came to him as he sat there with his head on his pillow books—an idea so perfect in its simplicity that he sat up straight and smiled. He went to the librarian and asked if he could get on the Internet; she told him where to sign and which computer to use. He was surprised at how quickly he was able to write the letter:

Hello,
    My name is Nick Taglio and I'm a sophomore
in high school. I've always wondered about
the other people who have screen names I
tried to get, and I was hoping you would help
me with a school project.

The class is called Diversity Workshop, and the assignment is to show how diversity affects our everyday lives. So I thought I would do a project that showed the diversity of people with a similar screen name. I was wondering if you would mind replying to this e-mail, answering these questions:

What is your name?

What made you use Nicktag or Tagnick in your screen name?

How old are you?

Are you male or female?

What is your occupation?

What is your ethnic background?

When did your ancestors first come to the United States?

He deleted the first question. People might not want to tell their names over the Internet to a total stranger. Of course, people might not want to give *any* of this information to a total stranger, but it was worth a shot. He wrote:

Anything else you might want to tell me about yourself would also be helpful in my report. Thanks for reading, and I hope to hear from you at your convenience.

Nicholas Taglio

"At your convenience"—*that was a nice touch,* he thought. The sort of thing a smart kid would write. In the subject line he put:

Then he sent the e-mail to Nicktag, Nickytag, Tagnick, Nictag and Niktag. He sent it to Nicktag52 and Nicktag73, and for good measure he threw in Nicktag1, Nicktag2 and Nicktag73000.

When the bell rang, he couldn't believe how fast the period had passed.


"You are going to kick that frog's ass tomorrow," Lucas said as they waited in the bus circle for Nick's mother.

It was dissection time in biology, and today Nick had not known the answer to a single question Mr. Shunk had asked about the invertebrate's innards. Lucas had offered to help, so after school they'd gone to the biology lab, taken their frog from the fridge and examined every gullet and gonad until Lucas was sure Nick had it all right.

"Could you believe Ariadne running out of the room"—Lucas flailed his arms, bobbed his head—"'I can't do it, I just can't!'"

"It *is* kind of sick, dude."

Lucas waved him off. "Oh, *please*. Get *over* it."

Nick laughed and huddled in his jacket. "She's *always* late."

"Are you sure your mom won't mind?"

"It's right on our way."

"Thanks. So . . . how *are* you, anyway? I mean, you *seem* better."

"Yeah, I'm better sometimes, and sometimes it feels like I'm . . ." Nick made his hand into a plane, going down.

"Well, two steps forward, one step back," Lucas said, all chipper.

Nick looked at him fast. "Do you know Kara Jensen?"

"Who's she, your new love toy?"

"No. Never mind." Nick balanced on the edge of the curb. "I miss skating," he mumbled.

"Yeah, and I hear they'll make the play-offs, for sure."

"Thank you," Nick said. "Thank you so much."

"Sorry," Lucas said in a little voice, with a little laugh. "But oh, Nick"—he spun around on one foot—"maybe you could become a figure skater!"

Nick responded with a burst of laughter.

"Like in that movie . . . oh, what's the name of it? D. B. Sweeney is an Olympic hockey player and he gets an eye injury and he has no peripheral vision, which I gather from the film is extremely important to hockey players?"

Nick nodded.

"But he *loves* to skate, so he becomes a *figure* skater!" The spin again. "How much do *you* love to skate, Nick?"

"Not *that* much, dude."

"Oh my God, it is *the* lamest movie. He's this blue-collar, salt-of-the-earth guy, and he pairs up with a super-rich bitch on wheels, and they fight, and then, of course, they fall in love," he said in a singsong, rocking his head side to side. "But it's worth it just to look at D. B. Sweeney for two hours. He is *so* my type."

"Thanks for sharing," Nick said, and Lucas, laughing, knocked him off the curb. The peeling Voyager pulled into the bus circle. "Here she is."

"Nice ride," Lucas said.

"Shut up."

"Shotgun!" Lucas yelled, and ran for the front door.

By the time Nick opened the slider, Lucas had already introduced himself to Nick's mom, who gave Nick a look of baffled amusement as Lucas was finishing: ". . . so he said you wouldn't mind because it's right on your way to the dentist."

"I don't mind at all."

Lucas started messing with the radio as she pulled into traffic.

"Just make yourself at home, Lucas," she said.

"Why, *thank* you, Mrs. Tag." He stopped where Five for Fighting was doing their sappy song about how Superman has such a hard life, because everybody expects so much of him.

"Oh, God, turn this off!" Nick protested.

"I *love* this song," his mother said.

"Me too." Lucas sat back and sang along:

*I'm only a man in a funny red sheet. . . .*

Lucas actually had a pretty good voice. . . . Maybe he was in chorus with Kara.

"Mrs. Tag." He leaned close to her, but spoke loud enough for Nick to hear: "This song *totally* reminds me of Nick."

"Oh yeah?"

Nick slumped down in the seat. "Oh . . . my . . . God."

"Seat belt, Nick," his mom said.

"You know the part where it says even heroes have the right to bleed? It's like, Nick thinks he has to be this big tough hockey guy all the time, but deep down—"

"Luke!" Nick sat up fast, clapping a hand on Lucas' shoulder. "Mom! Here's his corner!"

Lucas half turned, giving Nick a mock offended look. "It's *Lucas*," he said as Nick's mother pulled over. He extended his hand. Was the hearty handshake something you learned in smart-kid club? "Nice to meet you, Mrs. Taglio."

"It's been my pleasure, Lucas."

"*Do* you go by Mrs. Taglio?"

"Yes, I do. Thank you for asking."

Nick got out, to move into the front seat.

"I'm going to quiz you on IM later," Lucas warned.

"Okay. And, uh, thanks for the help."

Lucas raised his hand in a sort of backward salute as he walked off.

Nick shut the door. His mother drove off. "Nii—iiiick," she said in her best detective voice, "I *think* that boy is gay."

He gasped, shooting a look over his shoulder. "Lucas? You're *kidding*!"

She seemed alarmed—but then started to laugh, realizing he was putting her on.

"Good gaydar, Mom," Nick said. "Really, 'cause that was a *tough* one."

"All right, all right," she said, embarrassed, as they both kept laughing. Then she sighed, shaking her head. "Honestly, I can't figure you kids out. It's always faggot this, faggot that. Then you're like, 'Oh, here's Lucas, yawn.'"

"Lucas is gay," Nick explained. "But he's not a faggot. A faggot's a pussy. But you're not a faggot just because you're gay."

"Oh. But would you call *Lucas* a faggot to his face, like the rest of you do to each other?"

"Yeah, if he was acting like a faggot."

"Which is different from acting gay."

"Exactly."

"Thanks, it's as clear as mud now."

Nick looked out the window. It was weird—he had told Lucas about missing skating, something he hadn't told anybody else. Why Lucas? What had Nick expected? Some kind of sympathy, understanding? Some great pronouncement of truth? Instead, Lucas had done exactly what Nick would have done in the same situation: joked it off. So much for gay wisdom and sensitivity.

"Another stereotype bites the dust," he mumbled.

"What?" his mom asked.

"Nothing."

"Taglio!" Mr. P. called over the chaos that followed the final bell.

Nick turned; Mr. P. signaled him to come to the front.

"Am I chopped liver?" Mr. P. asked when the room was empty.

"Huh?"

"Earlier today, I had a little chat with my favorite student."

"And I thought *I* was your favorite student."

"Kara, your tutor."

"She digs you, too, Mr. P."

"She said you've started your diversity project—"

"*Started* being the operative word."

"—you're moving along in geometry—"

"Slowly."

"—and you dissected a frog with a fair amount of accuracy."

"Because Lucas dragged me through it."

"All of which leads me back to my original question: am I chopped liver?"

"Where'd that expression come from, anyway?"

"You're a pretty good writer, Nick," Mr. P. continued. "This paper should not be a problem for you. So, you're going to hand me a rough draft—when?"

"Mr. P., I gotta tell you, those topics—" He turned his thumb toward the floor.

"All right then, any topic. It doesn't even have to be about the book." He shrugged. "Whatever you want to write about."

"Well, that makes it even harder!" Nick protested. "*Any* topic—that's like 'Define the universe and give three examples.' "

Mr. P. just stared at him. "Nicholas. Write me a freaking paper. Write it about *The Old Man and the Sea*, write it about your baby brother, write it about the definition of the universe, just *get started*, okay?"

"Okay, okay." Nick backed away toward the door. "I'll try."

*Write it about your baby brother*. Maybe that wasn't a bad idea. Just tell some little story about Gabe and get it over with. . . . Distracted, he forgot not to walk out the front door—and he came face-to-face with the team, lounging on the steps as they waited for the bus to take them to practice.

"Dude," he and Griff both said, tapping their fists together.

"What up, Tag?" Ray asked.

He shrugged. "Not much."

Ramsey rambled over, hands in his pockets, wearing his preppie-jock-good-guy grin. "How you doing, Nick?"

"All right," Nick said, shaking hands.

"Where you been?" Jamie asked. "Don't you ever eat lunch?"

"I, uh . . . I go to the library."

"Library?" Steve hooted. "*You?*"

He shrugged again.

"Nicky Tag!" Deke strode over and got him in a brief headlock.

"Hey, Deke." Nick straightened up. "So . . . when's the game?" He knew exactly when the game was, but he was desperate for something, anything to say.

"Tomorrow night," Deke said. "We could use you there, dude."

"Yeah, with your mouth," Zach added, appearing beside Deke.

"We gotta get our side to drown out those West Shore jerk-offs," Steve added.

"I'm kind of buried with school shit," he mumbled. "Polinowski's up my ass for a paper."

"Party at my house after the game." Deke put on his earnest face, pointing at Nick. "Be there."

"Pretty confident, huh?"

Deke shrugged. "If we don't make the play-offs, it's my last game as a Cougar. And Zach and Cade and all the other seniors. So—we celebrate either way."

Nick nodded. "Yeah . . . I didn't . . . think of it like that."

The bus pulled into the circle.

"Good luck," Nick said. Translation: *I hope you get crushed.*

"Dinner's at my house, Tag," one of the juniors said. "If you want to come."

"Thanks."

They filed onto the bus, thumping him on the head, the back, the arm as they passed, just like when the EMTs were carrying him off the ice.

But if he hadn't run into them, nobody would have asked him to come to the game, or the party, or dinner. Then again . . . whose fault was that? They had tried, at the beginning. Maybe they'd just gotten sick of being told no.

As Nick started walking home, he wondered for the first time: what if it had been somebody else with the head injury? If Steve, say, had had to quit the team and he stopped coming to games and sitting with them at lunch, would Nick be going out of his way to include him? How well did he even know these guys? Would he even be friends with most of them if not for hockey?

But Griffin . . . that was another thing entirely. Today wasn't the first time he and Nick had both acted as if nothing had happened. Whenever they saw each other in the hall, they did the same thing, like a pair of machines: *Dude.* Hitting fists. Walking on. To ignore each other entirely—that would be acting like girls.

Nick wasn't even sure he remembered all that had been said at Griff's house that night. But he did know he'd been so wrapped up in his own misery, he'd lashed out at Griffin. Bad enough slagging him off about getting high. But that remark about lying on the ice and crying—he was lucky Griff hadn't flattened him. Then again: *Your same bad-ass macho game. Nicky Tag, the all-star with the Lindros style . . .* Griff had given as good as he got.

Maybe they were both wrong but too stubborn to admit it. Maybe they were both sorry, but neither one would tell the other for fear of looking like a woman.

# 39

The night of the game, Nick was working on his project. In the replies to his e-mail, he couldn't have manufactured such a diversity of Nicktags. Nictag was a Filipino woman in California. Nicktag52 was a Civil War reenactor from Louisiana, who called himself a Confederate American. Tagnick: lesbian bicycle store owner in Boulder, Colorado. Nicktag73: Russian immigrant in Philadelphia. Nickytag: college girl in Wisconsin, Norwegian descent. Niktag: guy in South Carolina with a clothing business, ancestors came from England in the 1600s. Nicktag73000: Latino in San Antonio, Texas.

As he pasted the e-mails into a Word document, he was vaguely aware of the phone ringing. Then his father ambled into the room wearing a stricken look.

Nick knew right away, but he said without expression: "What."

"They won."

Nick could just imagine it, Laura calling to warn them of the good news . . .

"Do you want to talk?"

"I'm good," Nick said, and went back to work.

But no more than half an hour later, he heard a car in the driveway, then Griffin's voice in the kitchen. What was this, *The Real World*, when he and Griff would have to have their emotional confrontation? Maybe Nick's parents could get it on video. . . .

"What up?" Griff asked, shambling into the room.

"Hey. How'd you do?"

"We, uh, won."

"I know. I meant, how'd *you* do?"

"Oh." He shrugged. "I sucked, actually. But Packard"—the opposing goalie—"sucked worse. Five to four."

Nick nodded. "Where's Maddy?"

"She, uh—she went ahead to Deke's."

Awkward silence. Nick gestured at his computer screen. "Diversity project."

"Yeah. We, um . . ." He shook his head, sighing. "After the game, Mac was giving the big victory speech and then he was all, like, 'There's somebody who helped us get here who couldn't be on the ice tonight, and I want to be sure nobody in this room forgets his contribution.' And I just . . . I felt like shit, Nick. You—"

"Is this what they call survivor guilt?" Nick interrupted, trying for an easy grin.

But Griff's answering smile was so genuinely sad, Nick had to look away.

"And after that," Griff continued, "Jamie and Steve and Ray were like, 'We're going to Tag's and getting him to come to the party.' And everybody else said, 'Do it, do it.' And I said, 'No, I'll go.'"

"Well, thanks," Nick mumbled. "But I can't. I got—"

"Finish it tomorrow."

Nick stared at the screen.

"Dude, this was your season. You were leading the whole pack. And I was an ass that night. You pissed me off, so I said things I shouldn't have, and—"

"Shouldn't've said, but still true," Nick muttered.

"Partly true," Griff muttered right back. "Only partly, and only sometimes. And that . . . some of that's jealousy from me, because I could never be the player you are."

"Were."

"Are."

Nick raised his eyes to Griff's.

"Come on. Shut it down and let's go." Griff grinned. "But first do something about your hair. It looks *really* disturbing."

When they were in the car, Griff said, "Nick, you probably figured this, but . . . I should tell you, Devin's gonna be there. And, you know, Ramsey."

But by now Nick was feeling so upbeat, so glad to be included and remembered again, he didn't even care. "Whatever."

Griff nodded. "Good," he said, and backed out of the driveway.

Deke's house had the perfect party setup, a huge lower level with a bar area and a room that opened onto the yard. He lived about two blocks from the beach. Tonight it was too cold for anybody to want to be outside for long, but as Nick and Griff approached the glass doors, laughter and music greeted them.

Alyssa was the first person Nick saw. Half bombed already, she threw her arms around his neck and kissed him on the mouth. "Nicky!"

"Hey, Lyss."

"I *miss* you, gorgeous. You're never around." She offered him a beer; he took it.

Cautiously, Nick looked around. No Devin in the vicinity. If he drank fast, it really wouldn't matter. He could talk to her. He could talk to anybody.

"Car keys, Mr. Burroughs," Deke's dad said. He winked at Nick, patting him on the back. "Hey, Nick. I'm glad we got you here."

"Hi, Mr. Con."

Griff handed over his keys. "I'm not gonna drink, though, Mr. Con."

"All well and good. If you don't drink, you can get 'em back later." Mr. Connelly drifted away.

"Hey, Tag." Deke grabbed him by the back of the neck.

"Congratulations," Nick said.

"We couldn't have done it without you. You know that, don't you?" Deke gave him the sincere captain gaze.

Nick shrugged. "Looks like you just did."

"Oh man, what a squeaker," Ray put in, joining them. "You should've been there, Nick. . . ."

And then it began, the play-by-play: who checked who, who got whistled, who won the face-off, who scored, who assisted, who dived, what jerk-offs the refs were, what jerk-offs the other team was, how slow the ice was. Everybody talked to Nick, everybody was glad to see him, but he realized with an ever-growing sick feeling that he could be nothing here but an audience.

Still, he laughed, and listened, and joked, and drank . . . and noticed that Devin was nowhere around.

And neither was Ramsey.

He told himself it couldn't be. He told himself he didn't care if it *did* be. He told himself Griff would've said something—and then he remembered: Devin's gonna be there, And, you know, Ramsey.

Nick felt dizzy and nauseated. He was suffocating. Mr. Dartmouth, with his Yale professor father, and Devin, with her little Cape Cod house like all the others on the street? No. Not possible . . .

"—and then Ray just charges in, knocks him off the puck, backhands it to Steve, and the next thing I know the red light's flashing!" Jamie was telling him. "It was just like that in-your-face goal you scored against Lourdes that time, remember?"

"Hey, Nick." The good-natured slimeball thumped him on the back, arriving from nowhere. "Good to see you."

Nick could tell by his friends' faces that he wasn't exactly hiding his contempt. He barely grunted in reply and mumbled something about getting another beer as he slipped away . . . and came face to face with Devin, still in her jacket, as he turned into the bar.

As soon as Nick saw that guilty, pouty face, he knew.

And he stared.

She tried to edge past.

He took her by the wrist. "You're with *him*?"

"Let go," she said.

"I want to talk to you." Why had he said that? He didn't want to talk to her. He wanted to slap her. He wanted to twist her arm until she cried.

"Nick . . ."

"Come outside and talk to me."

"Don't make a scene."

"Come out and I won't."

For the first time ever, she didn't give him an argument. Just whirled around and went outdoors. Nick took a beer from the refrigerator. Feeling like a zombie, he followed her onto the terrace.

"I can see whoever I want," was her opening shot.

"Are you fucking him?" Nick answered.

The word made her flinch; she turned her head away.

"You are?" he said, shaking with rage and jealousy.

"I don't have to answer to you, Nick."

"So, what was it, Dev? His money? His Land Rover? His phony charm? Because I can't believe it's all about hockey."

"Shut up, Nick. Just shut up," she said, and he was silenced by her quivering voice and glistening eyes. "You think you know everything, and you know what? You know nothing. Nothing!" She sobbed, once, and rubbed her eyes with the heel of her hand.

Nick took a long drink of beer. She started to walk past him, her head down. He blocked her path and said, "Tell me." His voice came out very calm, even—could it be?—gentle.

"Forget it," she said, pushing him aside.

And then Ramsey was behind Nick, saying, "Everything okay?"

Neither one answered him.

Ramsey said, "Devin?" The way he said it—like an annoyed teacher waiting for an explanation—made Nick want to plant a fist in his face.

Instead Nick just looked into Devin's eyes, then turned away.

He walked, coatless, through Deke's yard, heading for the beach, his head spinning, stomach churning. Before he'd gone very far, he heard Alyssa calling, "Nicky! Nicky!" She ran up behind him. "Oh honey." She wrapped an arm around his waist. "I'm sorry. You didn't know."

Nick didn't reply. They walked to the beach and sat on a stone wall, sharing Nick's beer. "What was *she* crying for?" he finally muttered.

Alyssa sighed. "It's complicated."

"Is that asshole hurting her in any—"

She cut him off fast: "*No*. No, nothing like that." She

squeezed his hand. "Tsss. Oh, that's sweet." Her tone of voice added: *You pathetic brain-damaged imbecile*. "It's just . . ." She sighed. "Cade's, you know, not all as perfect as he seems."

"*What* a surprise," Nick said bitterly. "So, then, why's she—" But he couldn't bring himself to say it again. "You know."

"Well, it's like . . . oh, I shouldn't be telling you this. But I'm so *mad* at her about it all, and anyway, you have a right to know, right?"

Did he?

But Alyssa didn't wait for his answer before continuing: "At first, like, she didn't want to? And—"

"At first being when?" Nick interrupted. He and Devin had split less than four weeks ago. Just how soon after abandoning his carcass had she moved on to fresh kill?

"Oh, about three weeks ago."

*That* soon. But she'd probably had it all plotted out in her devious little brain. He made a cynical laughing sound, shaking his head.

Alyssa kissed his cheek and rested her head on his shoulder. "Nick, aren't you *freezing*?"

"Keep going," he only said.

"They went out, like, twice, and he wanted her to do it, you know, right away. And she was like, 'No, I can't,' and all. So the third time they went out, she still wouldn't, and he was all, 'You have a decision to make.' He said she was being, quote, childish and controlling, and if she didn't, quote, get over it, there was no point in them being together. And then he said, 'Call me tomorrow and tell me what you want to do.' Then he took her home before her curfew."

"Oh my God," Nick said, deadpan. "Before curfew? The shame!"

Alyssa missed the joke. "I *know*. Her mom was all, 'Oh,

what's wrong? Is everything okay with you and Cade?' Because you know how her mom's, like, always in her business? Anyway, click on this link, she caved."

Nick drank some more beer.

Alyssa sighed. "Her and me had a huge fight about it. I was like, 'I can't believe you went groveling to him.' She was all, 'Who are *you* to talk? You've been with x number of guys.' And I said, 'Yeah, because I wanted to, not because they, like, forced me.' And she goes, 'No, no, he didn't force me,' and I'm like, 'Bullshit, Dev. You totally caved to his pressure and I *so* do not respect you for it.' And then she's all, 'Please don't stop being my friend,' as if I would, and just leave her in his power."

Then there was no sound but the breeze rustling dead leaves in the trees behind them. Nick stared at the reflection of moonlight on the water.

Alyssa finally said, "It won't last. A, Maddy and I think he's just using her to show off to his skanky Precious Blood girlfriend. B, he's so totally ivy-covered and Dev's so entirely not. And C, well—I don't even think she *likes* him all that much now that she has him."

Nick shot her a questioning look.

"Oh God. She'd go al-Qaeda on me if she knew I told you this. But screw it, Nick, she hurt you, and I think you have the right to know. The thing is, she doesn't even . . . I mean, you know, doing it with him, he doesn't . . ."

"I can't have this conversation," Nick said, jumping down from the wall.

But Alyssa was determined to finish. "She told me it was more fun with you."

He stopped and turned to her again.

"There." She shrugged. "I said it."

Nick drained the beer bottle. "And is that supposed to make me feel better?"

"It doesn't?"

Then they just looked at each other, as if they were total strangers.

Alyssa fumbled in her pocket and took out a pipe. "Come on. Smoke with me."

"Nah. I'm goin' home. And my mother, she's like one of those airport dogs." He sniffed frantically, jerking his head in all directions.

Alyssa laughed, then said, "Oh, don't go, Nicky."

"Yeah, I am." He started back toward Deke's house; she walked along. He tossed the bottle in a trash can.

"The thing is, Nick, here's my prediction. She's gonna want you back."

Nick stopped himself from laughing. Alyssa's intentions were good, but she was parked in a clue-free zone. "Lyss, what makes you think I'd *want* her back now?"

"Just because she slept with Cade?" Alyssa asked in a small voice.

They walked in silence as Nick mulled his answer. Then he said, "Not because she did it. But because of the reason."

After a pause, Alyssa said in a sort of awestruck whisper: "Yeah. Oh my God, I see what you mean."

In front of Deke's, Nick said, "Well, see you later."

"You're not . . . you can't *walk*, Nick!"

"Why not?"

"Because A, you're half bombed. B, it's miles to your house. And C, it's freezing and your jacket's inside."

"A, I'm only a quarter bombed. B, it's a mile at most. And C, I have no intention of going back in there." He kissed her cheek. "Bye, Lyss."

He hadn't gone two blocks when Griff pulled up to the curb, opening the passenger's window: "It's at least two miles, dickhead."

Nick got in and turned up the heat full blast. He put on his jacket, which was lying on the seat.

"I am *sorry*, Nick," Griff said. "I thought you knew."

"No big deal."

"I mean, that's why I said—"

"The brain-injured are a little slow at times. Forget it, dude."

Griffin drove. "Just so you know, Alyssa was totally discreet. She came up to me real quiet, and I got my keys back and left."

Nick nodded. "Okay."

"You want to drive around awhile? Go get a soda or something?"

"No. I want to go home and sleep, and I want you to go back and celebrate with your teammates."

At a red light, Griff sighed deeply and frowned, kneading his forehead with his fingers. "Nick. I got something to tell you. Before you hear it from somebody else."

Nick stared at him. What now?

"This is my last season. I told Mac. I'm done."

"What!" Nick practically yelled. "You're quitting?"

"I knew you'd—"

"Jesus, Griff, you've been working at this for eleven years!"

"Yeah, and that's why—"

"You're a *good* goaltender!"

"But I—"

"How can you just trash eleven years of your life, something you love and—"

"I *don't* love it!" Griff shouted, and Nick shut his mouth. "*You* love it, Nick. I don't! I've been telling you that for a couple of years, but you just blow it off!"

A car behind him honked; the light was green. Griff drove. "It's not fun anymore. It's just"—he shook his head—"not. And I feel bad, I do, quitting when you'd do anything to be able to play. But it's like Maddy said: 'You can't play for Nick.' You know? She sees what I go through every time I have to play, and—"

"What do you go through?" Nick asked quietly.

He saw Griff's fingers tighten on the steering wheel. "Dread." Griff swallowed hard. "Fear."

"Really?"

Griff nodded. "Ever since we started high school."

Nick tried to joke, doing one of their favorite lines from *Slap Shot*: "But you're a goalie. You're *supposed* to be like that."

Griff gave a weak smile. "I don't need it, you know? And, um, it's getting worse. I don't want to spend six months a year miserable for the rest of high school. Then feeling pressured to go to goalie camp in the summer. For what? It's not like I think I'm gonna play in college or anything. I feel like I'm stuck in this thing I hate just because I've been doing it so long. And I don't want to do it anymore."

"Maddy's okay with you quitting?" Nick asked after a silence.

"She's actually happy. *Really* happy."

"Because she knows how much you hate it."

"Yeah."

"What about your 'rents?"

Griff shook his head, grinning. "I swear to God, I thought my father was gonna cry. And my mother was like, 'But I'm supposed to be Booster Club president next year.'"

Nick laughed with him.

"I'm like, 'Well, go for it, Mom, I'm sure the team could use you!' And my dad's all, 'Maybe you could see a psychiatrist about this fear thing, Griffin.'"

"No!"

"I am *not* kidding. I said I don't need a shrink, I just need to get out of that cage. I'm just . . . I'm done. I've been thinking about it for two seasons now, and, okay, Hallmark moment: seeing you get hurt this last time . . ." His voice trailed off. He pulled into Nick's driveway. "And I think it's incredible, I really do, that you still want to play. I mean, I couldn't believe in November how you went back out there after a week and you were in everybody's face. . . ." He shook his head. "I was in awe, Nick. But it's different for me. I just don't love it. And you have to love it, don't you? Because it's so much work. If you don't love it, what's the point?"

"Yeah," Nick said. "So, what about the play-offs?"

"Oh, I'll play. Not that I really want to, but—you know, I can't let the team down any more than I already am."

"Steve giving you shit?"

"What do *you* think?"

Nick grinned.

"He's like, 'Griff, you faggot, leaving us high and dry.' I said, 'What do you care? With Nick and me gone, you and Jamie can be cocaptains senior year.'"

"So what're you gonna do with all this free time?" Nick asked.

"Who knows? Maybe get a job. Do a club or something at school. Something totally different, you know? And, um, I can hang out with my dickhead friend from time to time. Maybe we can even get a job together."

"Maybe." Nick opened the car door.

Griff said, "Nick?"

Nick looked at him.

"First round, we play Campton. Next Saturday, their ice. I was hoping . . . maybe you'd come and watch."

Nick gave a deep sigh.

"You know how it gets over there. With their fans."

"Yeah, but I—"

"Never mind," Griff said quickly. "It's just . . . it might be my last game. But—"

"It's really hard for me," Nick admitted. "No fun, you know?"

"Yeah, I know. Forget it. See you, dude."

"Thanks for the ride."

Griff looked at his dashboard. "Two point six miles."

"Oops," Nick said, and got out of the car.

His mom bustled toward the kitchen, singing out, "Hi, Bri!" When she saw it was Nick, her face fell.

He shrugged. "Sorry. Only me."

"Oh, I'm just . . ." She turned up her palms. "That was quick."

"Hey, Nicky." His dad scuffled in, wearing slippers and sweats.

"Hey." Nick took off his jacket.

"Everything all right, honey?" his mom asked with her sad little elfin face.

Might as well come clean. "Devin was there," he said casually. "With Cade Ramsey."

"Oh! That little bitch!" The elf morphed into a devil with eyes that shot fire.

Nick turned to his father, whose face was a mixture of horror and amusement. "Kaa-aath!" he said, and Nick couldn't help but laugh.

"I'm sorry!" She threw her hands up, bustling over to the sink. "I can't help it, that's how I feel!" She flung open the dishwasher and started loading the glasses that had been left on the counter. "And look at the time! I told Brian eleven-thirty, and what time is it now?"

Nick looked at the clock. Only 11:45? He felt like he'd been gone for hours. "You gave him an eleven-thirty curfew? That's a little *Happy Days*, isn't it?"

"I told her," his dad said, snickering. "Poor kid . . ."

"I don't care." She sounded defensive, but Nick could see she felt a little dopey, trying not to smile. "It's his first date. *I* don't know this girl."

"Mom, she plays an instrument," Nick said. "The kind with *strings*."

His parents looked at each other. "Is that some sort of code?" his dad asked.

Nick formed a halo over his head with his fingers.

"Oh," his mom said, and both parents started giggling.

"Well, I'm going to bed." Nick took an ice pack from the freezer.

"You okay, Nick?" his dad asked.

As Nick left the room, he said, "Headache—check. Dizziness—check."

"Too much beer at Deke's house—check," his dad called after him, and Nick laughed.

But as he went to the bathroom, washed his face, brushed his teeth, he found himself reliving every word between him and Devin, agonizing over how he'd looked to her, whether she'd thought he was pathetic or desperate or what. And then he moved on to what Ramsey thought of him, and what Ramsey might have said to Devin afterward. . . . All the while, he felt dread growing in his gut, knowing what was still to come.

Finally, in bed, he could no longer push away the disgusting images: Devin with Ramsey. Devin, who had been in this bed with Nick, basically naked. *She told me it was more fun with you.* Did Devin regret doing it with Ramsey? Now that she'd made the leap, did she wish she'd done it with Nick first?

He thought of her lying right here beside him, twisting her hair, wondering out loud why she couldn't have real sex with him. Then along came Ramsey and his scummy ultimatum . . . and Nick would never know why she had caved. It made him sick to think of Devin, proud, defiant Devin, calling Ramsey as he'd instructed her, saying . . . what? *Please come and pick me up, I'll be a good girl now and do whatever you say.* He couldn't help imagining what they'd done together. . . .

*Stop!*

Jumping up, he started pacing the room, clutching at his head like a mental patient. Finally he dropped down and did push-ups until he collapsed on the floor, lying with his cheek against the cool wood.

He heard a car in the driveway, then goodbyes, then Brian jogging up the porch steps.

*Gallant blowing curfew while Goofus comes home early?* Check.

*Best friend happily ditching the sport you're dying to play?* Check.

*Ex-girlfriend doing it with the guy you despise?* Check.

Skating, and the ice is big, much bigger than Nick has ever seen, and there's no noise from the crowd, no net, no goalie, no lines, and he's in a panic, his heart pounding, thinking, *Why is it so quiet? Where should I go? Who do I pass to? What do I do now?*

His eyes flew open.

Morning. He got up and looked out the window; the sun was just coming up over the neighbor's garage. He dressed in thermal underwear, pants, thermal shirt, hooded sweatshirt, socks and sneakers.

Then he took his skates from the closet.

Picking up his stick, he headed for the kitchen. At the back door he tied the skates together by the laces. He put on his gloves, pulled a hat over his ears and stepped outside. He walked down the porch steps—and up again, and back into the kitchen. On the countertop notepad he wrote:

At the garage, he opened the door slowly and quietly. His bike was way in the back, behind wheelbarrows and toboggans and summer furniture. So he wheeled Brian's out instead and propped it against the garage. He filled his sweatshirt pocket with pucks, draped the skates around his neck and rode out of the driveway, holding his stick across the handlebars.

It was only about a mile to Mallery's Pond. When he and Griff were younger they used to ride there all the time, meeting friends, staying all morning, grudgingly giving up the ice to families, then returning late in the afternoon. When the pond first froze, the ice was incredibly fast. As they rutted it with their stops and their sticks, it got bumpy and slow . . . but still fun. They made their own rules, called their own penalties. No such thing as offside, no boundaries. They just played for the thrill of the game.

But that was before travel team, before high school, when coaches didn't allow skaters to play on ponds for fear of injury. If you were going to get hurt, the coaches wanted it to be for *them*—not just because you were having fun. Even if they did allow it, who had the time? It was practice at the rink, every day after school, get on the bus and go to the ice, the clean, smooth, resurfaced ice. Games, tournaments, jamborees, skating clinics . . . You never stood at the pond's edge testing the strength of the ice. You stood at the boards waiting for the Zamboni.

What if he got there to find guys already playing—older guys who could never get indoor ice time? Could he play with them? Should he? It would be fun to play *Mystery, Alaska*-style again. But what Nick really wanted right now was to be alone on the ice.

The pond came into sight. . . . *Yes*. Empty.

Nick realized how out of condition he was when his legs wobbled beneath him. He sat on a rock and kicked off his sneakers, then slid his feet into the skates and laced them up. He had forgotten how good they felt. Top of the line, just about the best skates you could get . . . his parents had bought them for him.

His parents, who drove a peeling minivan and kept the house dark and cold to save on the CL&P bill, had spent $300 on new hockey skates this season. And they weren't even sure his feet had stopped growing. And they'd already been warned about the concussions.

As Nick started down to the ice, something Devin had once said popped into his head: *I like to watch you walk on skates*. Devin. With Ramsey. Why couldn't his brain be like a computer, where he could just define a thought and hit *Delete*?

He tossed a puck onto the ice and started out slow, dribbling it side to side, getting his rhythm. After a while, he picked up speed. The feeling was so good, it gave him a lump in his throat. The day was cold, but the sun was higher now, glistening on the ice.

> *When I skate, the whole world fades*
> *There are no Devins and no Cades.*

Nick laughed. He gathered some twigs and created a slalom drill, taking care to hold his head up, to keep the puck in the center of his blade. Then, making a goal from two rocks, he dropped pucks and took shots until his pockets were empty. He skated backward and forward, did crossovers and pivots. He did power starts and one-bladed stops and backward stops.

He skated to the far end of the pond, collected the pucks and turned around.

There was the whole empty pond, stretched out before him. Just like in the dream. No boards or lines or circles, no penalty boxes, no refs whistling, no fans screaming, no helmet echoes, nobody tap-tap-tapping their sticks looking for the pass. Nothing but . . .

"Open ice," he said.

*This* was what he missed the most. Not the cheers, the chaos, the goals. But the speed, the exhilaration, the freedom.

How could Griffin give this up? Probably because he was a goalie, always stuck in the cage, waiting for a puck to hit him, like a target in a carnival game. Maybe Griff didn't even remember what it was like to go sailing on his blades.

Then Nick dropped his stick, and he skated. He didn't charge along, but instead set a good, steady pace, stretching his legs, taking big strides, no need to worry about who was bearing down on him with evil intent. He just skated, while the wind cooled his face, and the sky swirled around, and his blades whispered *wish, wish, wish*.

Kara was reading his diversity project e-mails. She tucked a piece of hair behind her ear and bit down on a corner of her lower lip, the way Nick had noticed her doing whenever she was concentrating. Funny—she looked better every time he saw her. Not beautiful, but . . . appealing. He wasn't hot for her or anything, not at all. But maybe this was what they meant by the expression about beauty being in the eye of the beholder: The more you got to know somebody you liked, the better they looked to you.

Now she turned to him and smiled. "Nick, this is great stuff. It's almost like . . . you didn't make this up, did you?"

"You think I'm smart enough to make all that up?"

"Yeah, I *do*."

"Kara, I didn't even know Confederate Americans existed. And Tagalog, the language of the Philippines? What hat did I pull *that* out of?"

She laughed. "Dyer's going to love this. Now all you have to do is synthesize the information and hand it in."

"Synthesize?"

"Sort of draw it all together."

"You mean, like, comments and opinions?"

"Ooooh, scary," she said, holding out her arms and making her hands quiver.

"Shut up." He felt himself blushing as he took the papers from her.

"Write it up and I'll look at it, okay?"

"Okay, thanks."

"Oh, I almost forgot." She reached into her backpack and put two vitamin jars on the desk. "I got you these."

He picked one up. "Grape seed extract?"

"Yeah, and gingko biloba. I was doing some Web research about postconcussion syndrome, and I—"

"Oh, God," he said, rolling his eyes. "How do you get to *be* like that?"

She hit his arm. "I read that these two things can help. So why not give it a try? They're natural, they can't hurt you."

"That's . . . I mean . . . you didn't have to . . ." He turned away to stuff the jars into his backpack. "Thanks."

"You're welcome. Nick, are you all right? You seem kind of down today."

"Nah, I'm okay. Just tired, I guess." The skating had been great while it lasted, but he'd paid for it by spending the rest of Sunday on the couch, wiped out, dizzy—and depressed.

"Mmm," she said, and opened his math book.

"Actually . . ."

She looked up.

"I had some shit come down on me over the weekend. About hockey, and . . . this girl I used to be with."

"You feel like talking about it?"

Nick started drawing shapes in his notebook. "Well . . . Saturday night, when they made the play-offs? My friend

Griff, he's like my best friend since we were little, he, um, he comes to my house after the game and drags me to this party. Him and me were sort of not really talking before that, because we had this, like, fight about hockey."

"What do you mean?"

Nick hesitated—but then out poured the whole story of the night at Griffin's. He couldn't believe he was telling it; his mouth just kept moving, like he was controlled by a ventriloquist. Kara nodded, bit her lip, shook her head . . . listened. And he found himself segueing right into the party and Devin and Ramsey and his talk with Alyssa. He told her every last sickening detail.

"And you know what's so messed up?" he finished. "I actually found myself feeling sorry for *her*."

"That's not messed up, Nick. That's not messed up at all."

"Whatever," he mumbled, coloring in a rectangle.

"Of course it hurts now, and you're mad and you feel like a jerk, right?"

He nodded, twisting his mouth.

"But with all that—God, I think it's pretty amazing that you feel sorry for Devin!"

"Hey, I don't feel *too* sorry," he said. "I'm not Gandhi in a diaper here. I still want her to crash and burn."

"And it sounds like she will."

Nick stared at the desktop.

"Hey, here's something that might cheer you up." He raised his eyes; she touched her forehead. "Last week you wore a DMB cap. You're a fan?"

"*A* fan?" he repeated. "No. No, I'm *the* fan."

"My boyfriend would fight you for that title. Anyway, we got tickets to the Hartford show, at the Meadows, and now one of his friends can't go, so I was wondering—would you want to come? It's March fifteenth. A Friday."

See Dave? Live? Him? "Are you serious?"

"Some of us are driving up, and we're meeting the UConn people there."

See Dave? Live? Him? With seniors and college kids? In a car? Nick crashed to earth. "My parents wouldn't let me."

She looked puzzled. "How come?"

"You know—kids, cars, drugs, beer. Darkness. They'll picture themselves bringing my dental records to the coroner's office."

She laughed. "You mean they wouldn't even let you go with the academically accelerated?" Framing her face with her hands, she gave him a cheesy smile, batting her eyes. Now he was laughing. "*Ask* them."

"Oh, I *will*. Believe me."

"If they want, I'll talk to them. I mean, tell them I'll call them and—"

"Kara." He held up his hands: *enough*.

"Okay, okay," she said, and they finally got down to geometry.

"**Y**ou, um—you're not goin' to the game, are you?" Brian asked on Saturday as they sat on the kitchen stools waiting for their frozen pizza to bake.

"Nah," Nick said. "You?"

Brian shook his head; Nick could tell he was staying away from the play-offs out of a sort of solidarity.

"What're you up to, then?"

"Oh, I'm goin' over Emma's. We're gonna work on our social studies projects."

"It's Saturday night, Bri."

"Well, I want to get mine done before March Madness starts. And besides—we're gonna use the Internet." He opened the oven and checked the pizza too carefully. "In her rec room. In the basement."

"Why, June, I believe the Beaver is growing up," Nick said, and Brian laughed. "So you really like this girl?"

"Yeah. A lot."

Nick nodded. "Listen. Don't try to, um, you know, go too fast or whatever."

Brian turned slowly, staring at Nick in amazement.

"Shut up," Nick said, pointing at him. "Just shut up and listen. You got time . . . for all that. Just take it slow and everybody'll be happy."

"Nick, you're scaring me," Brian said with a grin.

The door rattled, and their mom came in with Gabriel and a Wendy's bag.

"I gah fwench fwies," Gabe announced, pitching himself at Brian.

Brian swung him upside down as Gabriel shrieked happily.

"How come *he* gets Wendy's?" Nick asked.

"Nicholas—when I buy him Wendy's, it's a two-dollar kiddie meal. When I buy you Wendy's, it costs me eight dollars. Here." She held out a french fry.

"Sporting," Nick grumbled, but he ate it.

His father got home a couple of minutes later, and they all sat in the dining room with pizza and Wendy's and left-over meat loaf.

Everybody was in a pretty good mood, for once, so Nick said casually, "Oh, you know my tutor? Kara? She has tickets to Dave Matthews in a couple weeks. Up in Hartford. She asked me to go."

"Whoa!" Brian said. "You're going to the Meadows to see DMB?"

"Well, if—" He waved his hand at his parents.

"In a motor vehicle?" his mother said. "At night? With humans of the teenage variety? Dream on, Nick."

"They're not like *me*. This is Kara and her friends. God, they probably keep both hands on the wheel!"

Brian laughed.

"Come *on*," Nick said.

"Kath?" His father shrugged. "It's DMB."

She sighed defeat.

"Score," Nick said. "Thanks!"

"You'll call us as soon as you get there, and as soon as it's over," his dad said. "How many people are going?"

"Not sure, but I'll get their Social Security numbers so you can run the check."

"Dad, can you drive me to Emma's?" Brian asked, getting up.

"Can I have five minutes to finish my dinner?"

"Take ten." Brian clapped him on the back and headed out of the room.

"When are we going to meet this girl?" their mom called.

"Yeah, okay!" Brian jogged up the stairs.

"Have *you* met her, Nick?" she asked.

"Never even seen her."

His dad cleared his throat in the way that announced: *I am about to say something of grave significance.* "Nick. Are you, uh, thinking about going tonight?"

"Nope."

"It's just that . . . Jack seems to think Griffin would really appreciate it."

Nick didn't answer.

"And with the possibility of its being his last game and all—"

"And whose decision was that?" Nick slid his chair back from the table.

"Nick, you can't just walk away every time you don't want to face—"

"There's where you're wrong," Nick interrupted. "Because, see? I can," he said, and left the room.

✳ ✳ ✳

In the den he lay on the couch, flipping through the channels. He bypassed the Rangers game, but there was nothing else to watch, so the second time around, he stopped. Could he take it?

The Rangers were playing the Flyers—Lindros' old team. This could be entertaining. Lindros was mucking it up in the corner with a Flyer defenseman.

"Look at Lindros, John," said one of the announcers.

"He is *really* playing a physical game tonight, Joe," John answered.

"Yeah, but you know what else struck me? It looks like he's finally learned his lesson about holding his head up."

"I think you may be right about that, pal."

The Rangers were on a power play. Lindros redirected a Mike York slap shot and tipped it in. The red light flashed and Eric's stick went up.

"Oh! Score!" Joe yelled. "Oh, this has *got* to be sweet for Lindros, scoring twice against his old team!"

Twice? His second goal of the game? Eric skated along the Ranger bench, getting his helmet tapped by teammates.

"And, you know, Joe, after the concussion in December, there were plenty of people who said Lindros should just flat-out never play again."

Just then York jumped on a terrible pass by the Flyers' Jeremy Roenick. York passed to Lindros, and—"One timer in for the goal!" Joe shrieked.

"Hat trick, Eric Lindros!"

Nick got up and stood right in front of the TV, gluing his eyes on Lindros. The camera zoomed in on his grin as the Rangers circled him.

"Oh my gosh, John, what a coup for Lindros! He's only had four goals total since the December concussion, and now three in one game!"

"And against the Flyers—can you *measure* that kind of satisfaction?"

Now Eric was on the bench, watching the game.

And Nick was turning off the TV, walking to his room.

He changed into black pants and a white shirt, black socks and shoes. He chose a tie and stood in front of the mirror.

"It looks like he's finally learned his lesson about holding his head up," Nick said, turning up his collar. And he replied, "I think you may be right about that." Carefully, he knotted the tie. He took a deep breath and blew it out again.

He found his team windbreaker in the back of the closet and put it on, then went to the living room. His dad was on the floor with Gabriel, playing trains. His mom, who had been reading a book, just stared at him.

"Dad?"

He raised his head.

"Would you . . . do you mind driving me to Campton?"

He looked stunned, but he got up right away. "Sure, Nick."

"Dad-*dy*!" Gabriel complained.

Nick's mom slid to the carpet. "It's okay, Gabey. Mommy will play with you."

His dad headed for the kitchen.

"See you," Nick said to his mom.

"Nicky?"

He turned back with a suspicious look.

"Don't worry," she said. "I won't say anything stupid, like I'm proud of you."

"*That's* a relief." Nick suppressed a grin as he left the room.

In the car it was quiet until Nick said, "Thanks. About the concert."

"No problem."

Nick thought for a while about how to set up the next couple of things he wanted to say. He planned it like a play: *I'll go here, he'll go there, then I'll take the shot. . . .*

"Lindros scored a hat trick just now."

"Oh yeah? You were watching the game?"

"Uh-huh."

"A hat trick against the Flyers. Wow, he must be loving that."

"Yeah. And he only had four goals, total, since his last concussion."

His father didn't answer; Nick could tell he was figuring out where this was heading. That was the problem with planning plays. Usually the opposition had ideas of their own.

Time to rush the goal: "And I started thinking, the thing about Lindros is, he never comes back till he's ready. But he always comes back."

His father sighed. "Nick, do we really have to have this fight again?"

"I'm not fighting. I'm just saying."

"And what is it, exactly, that you're saying?"

"I'm not gonna be sixteen forever."

Silence.

Nick looked out the window. "I'm not trying to be a jerk. Really. But I just . . . I realized that in two years, it's gonna be my decision, right? I'm gonna have to be the one to negotiate the world, just like you said. And I don't know what I'll do then, you know? How I'll feel, or"—he shrugged—"maybe by the time I'm eighteen I won't even be able to make up the lost time. But I've been thinking about Griff. How for him, quitting is the right thing to do. And for me, it's not. I *can't* let it go. At least . . . not yet."

"Okay, Nick." His dad's voice was quiet. "Okay."

"But, um, also? I'll go for those tests and the rehab and all that. Whatever I have to do to get back to a hundred percent. Or what passes for a hundred percent with me."

"You know, Nick, you make a lot of comments like that. I hope you realize it's all bull. You're every bit as smart as Brian."

"No I'm not."

"Yeah you are. But it's like . . . you think you can't be, because it's not cool."

Just like Lucas: *Nick thinks he has to be this big tough hockey guy all the time.* And Kara: *Your teachers might actually believe you're smart.* And Griff: *If you love hockey so much, how come you kept playing your same bad-ass macho game?*

Last winter, when all the hockey camp and power-skating brochures had come pouring in, one was from a woman whose specialty was teaching you how to fall properly when you get checked. Even though it came with endorsements from NHL players, Nick had just shaken his head and tossed the brochure aside. He could take the hits. He didn't need anybody, especially a woman, to teach him how to fall.

But violence in hockey—it was kind of like what Twain said about the weather: everybody talks about it, but nobody does anything about it. There was just no denying that hitting *was* a big part of the game. He could learn to keep his head up, to be less aggressive. But Blakeman was right: he would still get hit. So if he was serious about playing again someday, maybe this woman's program was the place to start.

He wouldn't bring it up now, though. He'd said enough for tonight. The seed had been planted.

Now he would let it grow.

In a TV movie, the final scene would start with music swelling as Nick burst triumphantly through the doors of the Campton rink. Devin would run to him, throwing her arms around his neck. His old teammates would swarm off the ice and mob him, while Ramsey stormed off in the other direction.

Then Coach Mac would wade through the crowd to get to him, and even the Campton players and fans would break down and cheer. . . .

Nick's stomach tightened as he walked into the building with his dad, their steps echoing in the empty cinder-block lobby. This place had seen the Cougars' nastiest battles and toughest defeats. The Cougars were hated here—and they hated in return.

"You okay?" his dad asked.

"Uh-huh," Nick said, but he felt like his mouth was stuffed with cotton.

"I'm gonna sit with the parents."

Nick nodded. "Don't leave without me. I'm coming home with you."

His dad smiled. "Okay."

The teams were on the ice, midway through stretches and warm-ups. Griffin's cage was way at the opposite end; Nick walked on the side that was free of bleachers.

As he turned the curve where the Dragons were warming up, somebody slammed into the boards right next to him. He jumped; the Dragons were highly amused. Nick, feeling hot and light-headed, kept walking.

"Hey, Taglio!" A Dragon defenseman skated backward alongside him, holding four fingers right up to the glass. "How many fingers do you see?"

"Just this one," Nick said, flipping him off.

As he crossed the red line his own teammates started to notice him.

One at a time, they skated to him, hitting their sticks on the glass. No show. No stops. No words. A quick tap, then back to work. Steve, Deke, Ray, Jamie, Zach, every guy on the team . . . even Ramsey.

Griffin was the only one who didn't see him. When Nick was directly parallel to the goal he stood and watched Griff doing his stretches, skating his little patch of ice, trying to get his head right, shutting out everything else.

Finally Jamie skated past Griff, saying something, and Griff looked up fast, jerking his head to the right. When he saw Nick he grinned like a five-year-old and skated toward him.

Nick raised his fist to the glass.

Griffin tapped the glass with his blocker glove and skated away again.

# OVERTiME

"Taglio!" Mr. P. yelled at the end of the day.

Nick turned.

Mr. P. tapped his desk.

"I know, I know—your paper. I'll get to it tonight. I swear to God."

"Uh-uh," Mr. P. said. "You'll get to it right now."

"What!"

Mr. P. shrugged. "I have nowhere to go. Do you?"

"No, but—"

Mr. P. pointed to a desk.

"Come on, Mr. P. I'm tired. I have a headache."

"Tell it to your neurologist."

Nick was getting annoyed. It had definitely been a one-step-back day, and he wanted to go home. Teachers were supposed to give notice before assigning detention—and this *was* detention, wasn't it? Sullenly, he slid into a chair.

"I'm not asking you to turn in anything," Mr. P. said. He walked to the door and shut it. "All I want is to see the kind of good-faith effort you've been showing all your other teachers."

"So you're gonna hold me prisoner until I write something?"

"Don't think of it as being held prisoner," Mr. P. said cheerfully, strolling toward his desk. "Think of it as me providing a quiet refuge in which you can begin a long-overdue assignment." He sat down and pulled his chair in.

"I can't create under duress," Nick said, and Mr. P. burst out laughing.

"Taglio, get out your cell and call your mom. What do you call it in hockey, when you play till somebody scores?"

"Sudden death."

"Tell her we're in sudden-death overtime. We'll be here till one of us wins."

Nick didn't call. Mr. P. started grading papers. Nick slumped in the chair and stared at him, but Mr. P. kept working away.

Nick folded his arms and sighed loudly. Finally Mr. P. looked up, giving him a questioning look.

"You don't know what it's like," Nick mumbled. "To lose the thing you've been working at since you were five. The thing you love most. And having your head screwed up and not knowing if you'll ever be totally right again."

Mr. P. got up slowly, picking up a white legal pad. He walked to Nick and slid the pad toward him. "As they say on those realistic police dramas"—he slapped a pen on the paper—"write it."

Then he went back to his desk.

Okay. He was serious. *Just write something, anything, and get out of here fast.* . . . A good-faith effort. Any topic.

Well, Nick could write about the game, how he'd gone and stood by Griff's goal the whole time, ducking outdoors in between periods so he wouldn't have to talk to anybody.

Stood and watched, just so Griff would know he was there. Watched Ramsey score. Watched Devin jump up and down. Watched Griffin play one of the best games of his career, shutting out the Dragons 2–0 to advance the Cougars to the next round. Watched the team mob Griffin at the final buzzer, carrying him off the ice as Nick stood there in his shirt and tie, then went home in the Chevy Cavalier.

He could write about that, but—it would be too pathetic. It would make him look noble and unselfish, and that wasn't how he'd felt at all. Besides, if Mr. P. thought Nick was going to write some whiny paper about concussions and hockey, he was sadly mistaken.

Nick picked up the pen and tapped it on the desk over and over, watching. If the noise annoyed Mr. P., he didn't let on. Nick put his thumb on top of the pen, clicking the ballpoint in and out about twenty times, fast. Still, Mr. P. didn't even look up.

For a long time, Nick just stared at the white surface and the blue lines. Finally he started to write:

*In the dream, there's always open ice. . . .*

# Acknowledgments

Special thanks to Debbie Raccio, who for fifteen years shared the details of her family's hockey life; to Sam Hughes, for always being my insightful first reader; and to Colleen Kunz, who unintentionally gave me the idea for this book.

**Pat Hughes**, a Connecticut native, lives in Narbeth, Pennsylvania. A copy editor at the *Philadelphia Inquirer*, the author is married and has two sons.